BAGGAGE

Laura Barnard

Julie,

So glad you're enjoying the series!

Love + Laughs

Laura Barnard

x x x

First Edition

A CIP catalogue record for this title is available from the British Library.

Dedication

This book is dedicated to my mum, Lorraine. I appreciate your help and encouragement, even if I don't say it every day. x

Prologue

2005

I can't believe the week is over. It's easily been the best week of my life. I feel terrible saying that, considering it's all because of a boy. Just some stupid boy. Some stupid boy with floppy hair, bronzed skin and the most adorable freckles. I miss him already. How is that even possible?

I can tell he's going to miss me too because last night our stolen kisses were that much more urgent. Not that we talked about it. That would be having to admit we like each other and honestly, I don't know if he really does or if he's just playing me. I mean, why would a gorgeous specimen like him be interested in plain, little, flat chested me?

I've helped Dad load the last bits into our car boot and I still haven't seen Jack, even though his dad's been loading his car which is right next to ours. Now my dad's shaking his dad's hand. Shit, this is it. We're going.

Mum's locking up the caravan. If I go without seeing him it's possible I'll cry the whole way home. Just then his mum appears, him following behind with his brother. Everyone starts saying loud goodbyes, sharing hugs. Jack and I stare at each other awkwardly. I look at the adults, super aware that they'll notice if we show any emotion towards each other and rib us the whole way home.

'So... I'll see you then,' I say with a shy smile.

'Yeah,' he smiles. 'I'll see you.' He smiles sadly before turning to face towards our parents.

I'm gutted. He's just dismissed me like that? After all this time.

That's when I feel it. His index finger curls around mine. It's so subtle no one else would notice, but it warms my heart through. I squeeze it back.

'Come on kids. Time to hit the road.'

And just like that he was gone.

Chapter 1

Thursday

Erica

'You are such a slut,' I say to Brooke, jokingly punching her on the shoulder. 'Stop looking at every guy in here like they're a piece of meat you want medium rare.'

Brooke's always on the hunt. Ten days on Luna Island, in a bikini which showed off her bodacious body, was only going to add fuel to the fire.

She rolls her eyes. 'Will you stop looking for their deep meaningful personalities? I've told you, all men are twats. That's why you have to find the best parts, if you know what I mean.' She waggles her eyebrows suggestively.

'Trust me. There's a woman three floors up that knows what you mean.'

I'm no prude, but Brooke always seems to be able to

make me blush in public. You'd think five years of sharing a flat with her would've got me used to her, but I'm always checking to see if people can hear us.

Our friend Molly insisted we went on this last minute holiday to give us a much needed break in the sun. My mum's been having chemo for breast cancer and when I go back we're celebrating her last round.

'Phwoar,' she purrs, gazing towards reception. 'It seems we're in luck. Some boy toys just arrived.'

I roll my eyes but follow her gaze to see a group of lads about our age walking in with suitcases. They're the only people we've seen our age so far. Everyone else seems to be in their sixties plus. We were beginning to think this place was only advertised in old people's homes.

That's when I spot him. All chocolate brown hair, and hazel eyes. I freeze; my heart dropping out of my knickers, as the room whirls around me. My head feels like it's floating to the ceiling. It can't be...right? But the feelings bubbling up in my chest and the longing between my legs tell me a different story.

It's Jack.

Fuck.

I duck to the floor as if I've heard a gunshot. I can't see him. He *cannot* see me like this. I'm only in a bikini with a see-through kaftan thrown over the top. My hair is gathered in a messy bun on the top of my head and my face is completely free of make-up. This *cannot* be happening.

'Jesus, Erica. What the fuck is wrong?' Brooke whispers, trying to drag me back to standing. It's pretty rare that I embarrass *her*.

'That's...that's...' My voice is high pitched and wobbly. I'm really struggling to hold it together right now. Please, God, say this is a nightmare.

'Jesus, spit it out!' she snaps, her ice blue eyes wide in disbelief.

'That's...Jack,' I manage eventually, my tongue shaking so much it's hard to talk.

Her eyes narrow on me. 'Jack who?'

She's *seriously* dumb.

'Jack! The caravan-park-teenage-romance-first-fucking-sexual-experience-Jack!'

Jeez, just saying it out loud brings back a flood of memories I've desperately tried to forget.

'*That* Jack?' she screeches, so loud it echoes off the marble walls. Her head turns towards the door and she gulps. This can't be good.

'Did...you just call me?' a deep manly voice asks from nearby.

Just hearing his voice again makes me quiver. I *have* to get out of here. Hide somewhere. I crawl under a table and prise my hands together praying for death. Come on God: I recycle, I floss my teeth, I'm a good bloody person, dammit!

'Err...' Well, this is a first. Brooke's never lost for words.

A couple come to sit on the table and their legs kick me, attacking my ribs from both sides. I yelp, smashing my head on the top of the table.

'Is that...' his voice comes again, closer now.

Oh my fuckety fuck. I scrunch my eyes shut, hoping and praying this isn't really happening. This could be a nightmare, right? This could just be the worst nightmare ever. Something this horrendous doesn't happen in real life...does it?

When I pry one eye open I see Jack's gloriously beautiful face leaning down, peering at me hiding under the table, his mouth wide open, eyes nearly popping out of his skull.

My heart stops as I take him in. He's still got the same brown messy hair that's just that bit too long and falls over his forehead, almost into his eyes. And those eyes. The eyes from my dreams. They're neither hazel nor green, just a strange colour in between.

'Erica?' he gasps from his beautiful plump, pink lips that I immediately want to jump up and bite.

'Jack!' I exclaim, smashing my head on the table

again. Ouch. *Way to play it cool Erica.*

He grimaces, as if noticing how much that must have hurt, before offering his hand. His large, used to touch me all over, hand. I look at it with trepidation. *He's only offering to help you up, you bumbling idiot.* I take it, feeling the same burn his touch always left on my skin, and let him lift me to standing.

My God, how is it fair that he got hotter? I've always kind of hoped that he was one of those gorgeous teenagers that peaked early and was now obese and ugly, possibly bald. But this level of good looking, well it's just not fair at all.

'What are you doing here?' he asks, putting his hand through his hair and messing it up further. Holy moly, I want to do that.

I stare back at him dumbly, mesmerised by the beauty of his face. How has he not been scouted by a model agency by now? Maybe he has. Maybe he's shooting here on location.

'Your mate's not the sharpest pencil in the case, is he?' Brooke chuckles.

I look up to see three of his friends looking between us both, puzzled. I take a discreet deep breath, trying to pull myself together.

'Oh...hi,' I mumble, awkwardly waving. I am *such* a geek.

For heaven's sake, why couldn't I be wearing make-up right now? Just a bit of blusher, maybe a slick of concealer to cover the dark circles under my eyes from our long flight. I must look horrendous. Don't get me wrong, I'm not completely uggers, but always suffer from redness on my chin regardless of whether I'm having a breakout or not.

I force myself to concentrate and take in their names as he introduces them.

'This is Nicholas.'

Fucking *yummy*. He's tall and slim but with lean tattooed biceps that I'm sure could throw you across the room. In fact, his arms are completely covered in them all the way down to his fingers. I wonder if he has more underneath his basic black t-shirt.

He's got light brown hair which is waxed into a stylish quiff. It makes me almost giggle that his whole brooding, moody look is clearly supposed to show how unbothered he is. But that hair is a different story. He must have spent ages doing that quiff.

'Tom.'

Tom is what I'd call typical, standard good looking: all big broad shoulders, blonde short hair and piercing green eyes. He smiles, appearing friendly, if not a little flirty. I can already see him eyeing up Brooke. She's basically writing her telephone number with her tongue.

'And you know Charlie.'

Wow, *this* is Charlie? His lovely and hilarious best friend. I remember him from all those years ago. He's put on some weight since then. It doesn't help that he's shorter than everybody at about five eleven. He's got a few double chins and a pot belly, but he's still well put together in a polo shirt, shorts, and converse.

'This is Erica,' he says to them with a shy smile, a hint of a blush on his cheeks.

They all nod, but recognition washes over Nicholas and Charlie's faces.

'No way! How are you, Erica?' Charlie asks, stepping forward to dramatically bring me into a bear hug, swaying me from side to side. 'You're looking even more beautiful than your teenage self.'

'Thanks,' I giggle. I always loved him. 'My boobs finally came in,' I grin jokingly.

He nods, looking over them appreciatively. 'You're telling me!' he cries in mock shock, eyes widening to double the size.

Brooke clears her throat, clearly feeling left out.

'Oh, and this is Brooke.'

'Hi guys,' she smiles, faking a coy look as she pulls her long black hair over one shoulder and pretends she needs to adjust the straps on her string bikini.

Their eyes immediately go to her boobs. Not her first

rodeo.

I smile shyly back at Jack. He holds the back of his neck, his head tilted down, but his eyes watch me. He seems mildly amused by the situation. I do my best to smile back coyly, but can't help but feel awkward.

He looks at me a bit strange, a wrinkle forming between his eyebrows. He must think I'm a right dog looking like this. Just how you want to bump into your ex boyfriend, not.

I have no idea how much time has passed, but suddenly Brooke is pulling me away, shouting back to them 'see you later.'

I shake my head, trying to snap myself out of my daydream. 'See them later?' I repeat, blinking, still dazed.

'Yes, you smitten kitten,' she cackles. 'We're meeting them later at the bar. Give us a chance to show ourselves off all dressed up.'

I beam widely. I still can't believe this is happening. My Jack. Here. With me.

She grimaces. 'Oh babe, sorry but you've got a bit of broccoli in your tooth from lunch.'

Chapter 2

Jack

I can't believe she's here. My Erica. And damn, did she get hot! Not that she wasn't before, but now she's show-stoppingly beautiful. Her friend Brooke's not bad either.

'So, who was that?' Tom asks as we walk towards our rooms.

'Sort of a long story,' I say on a sigh.

'So, she's an ex, right?' he presses, face lit up in amusement. He's always been a nosy bastard.

'Yeah, an ex,' I nod with a shrug.

Charlie gives me a knowing smile.

'Right,' Tom nods. 'So, is she fair game?'

Is he fucking joking? I turn to glare at him, my jaw clenched.

'Are you fucking kidding me?'

He chuckles, putting his palms up in surrender. 'Hey

man, just because she's an ex doesn't automatically mean she's yours. Are you still into her or something?'

I've never *not* been into her. I just fucked it up because I was a proud twat back then.

'Or something,' I snap, my muscles feeling tight. 'Just stay the hell away from her, okay. The last thing she needs is Tom "Man Whore" Maddens getting all up in her face.'

'Yeah, leave it out Tom,' Charlie warns, attempting to open our door with a key card. He turns to me with a secretive smile. 'She's the one that got away.'

My nostrils flare. 'Shut-up,' I snap, attempting to cover it up by giving him a playful shove. Even though he's right.

'She's the one you told me about once,' Nicholas says with a knowing nod. Shit, I forgot about that. Too much tequila at Barry's 30th. 'What are the odds of her staying in the same resort?'

'Pretty slim,' I admit with a huge grin. I hope she's here for the whole week too. It would suck if she's leaving tomorrow or something.

'Some would say its fate,' Charlie grins, finally opening our door.

God, he's a soppy bastard. Always has been.

'Ooh, Jack's in L-O-V-E,' Tom sings playfully, shoving me into my room.

I push him back and slam our door behind him. I could do without him trying to wind me up right now.

'It's good to see her, though, right?' Charlie asks, bouncing excitedly from foot to foot. 'I saw your face when you realised it was her. You're still into her.'

I sigh, rubbing my face with my hands. 'I was never truly out.'

Erica

I can't believe that's him. My Jack. What are the chances that he'd be on the same holiday as me? It must be like one in a million. All our memories are invading my mind, making me feel as giddy as a teenager.

I still remember the very first time I saw him. My parents had dragged me and my brother to a caravan park in the summer holidays. I was so fed up that I couldn't stay back with my friends or at least go on a cool holiday abroad. We were having breakfast in the clubhouse when I looked around the red wallpapered room, crammed with far too much mahogany furniture. That's when I noticed him.

At first I was shocked there was anyone else there around my age. At fifteen, I wasn't the normal clientele of eight year olds. He was rolling his eyes at something his mum had said. He was stunning.

He had the most beautiful golden skin, with a smattering of freckles over his nose and under his eyes. His dark brown hair fell in curtains with half grown out sun-in blond hair. For some reason, it didn't stop me fancying him.

He looked up and caught me gawking at him. I was so embarrassed, quickly looking down, pretending to scan the menu. When I chanced a quick glance up I found him smiling at me. Not an overly flirtatious smile. A shy, unassuming smile. And just like that I knew my holiday had just become a whole lot more interesting.

Brooke rushes me back over to the girls who are lounging around the pool. Brooke's telling Molly and Alice all about it. She's trying to tell Evelyn too, but she's too busy staring at me, her eyes wide as if to say *really?*

The annoying thing with Evelyn is that she can say so much more with her dark brown eyes than if she were to talk. I know exactly what her accusing stare is saying.

Don't tell me we're gonna go through this again. That's what they're asking, prying into my soul.

'What about Karl?' Molly asks me with a grimace.

Ah, yes. The boyfriend back home that I've been trying to dump for the last two months.

'What about him?' Brooke snorts. 'I've been telling her to dump that dweeb for ages.'

I roll my eyes. 'Brooke, you know that's not fair.

He's really been there for me since Mum got diagnosed.'

I know I wouldn't still be with Karl if my Mum hadn't been diagnosed with breast cancer after our second date. It kind of fast-forwarded our relationship. I needed someone to lean on and he was there for me. He'd been absolutely brilliant, there when I needed him, but not crowding me. Exactly how I liked it.

So then why have I been thinking about finishing it with him the last few months? *Because he's boring.* Bloody hell, that's an awful thing to think. I'm such an ungrateful cow. But...well, the feelings aren't there.

I've been trying to bring it up for the last few months, but he seems oblivious to it and I feel too awful to dump him. Instead I've been doing the really douchey guy thing of treating him badly, hoping he'll dump me. I'm such a chicken shit.

'That might be true,' Alice agrees, 'but let's be honest. You've never been that into him. It's obvious for anyone to see.'

I sigh, a wretched guilt settling deep within my stomach. 'I know, but how on earth can I dump him just when my Mum's at the end of her chemo? After he's been there for me. He's done absolutely nothing wrong. It's not his fault.'

'I think he's sweet,' Molly says, her forehead furrowed.

'But if she doesn't feel it in her lady parts there's no point,' Brooke snaps, matter of factly.

If it was up to that I would never have gone on a second date with him.

I can sense Evelyn staring at me, but I'm trying to avoid it. It's like I can feel her eyes on me like hot laser beams. She's really pissing me off. Why can't she just be excited and giggly like Molly? Or straight-laced, asking loads of questions like Alice. Not all judging. My irritation begins to spike and before I know it I'm barely able to conceal my rage towards her.

'Go on then, say it!' I bark, shocking the other girls into silence. 'Say what you're gagging to say.'

She leans back in her sunlounger, sipping on her colourful cocktail. 'What exactly do you want me to say?' she asks, as cool as a cucumber. Gosh almighty, she's infuriating.

'What do you think she should do about Karl?' Alice asks, chewing on a straw.

Evelyn rolls her eyes. 'The question we should be asking is if we'd even be having this conversation if Jack hadn't just walked into the hotel.'

Urgh, I hate when she's so cocky! You see Evelyn and I go *way* back. We've been besties since primary school and because of that she knows everything about me. She's been through all the highs and the lows. The lows are the problem with this case. She's remembering how I was when it all went to shit with Jack. How I would pretend I was okay at school, only to go home and cry myself to sleep while watching Sleepless in Seattle. God, I love that movie.

But she has no reason to tell me what to do. Whatever I want to do it's my life and she needs to realise that. Am I excited and ridiculously giddy over seeing him again? Of course! Any normal human being would be. Am I going to jump into bed with him again? No! I have a boyfriend. Yeah, I might be planning on dumping him when I get home, but I'm still currently attached and I abhor cheating.

I won't be sleeping with him. Well...Maybe not. Oh, who could guess at this stage. All I know is that the butterflies that have been lying dormant in my stomach have come back to life, flying around screaming *'He's here! He's here!'*

'I know you're going to say that I shouldn't go near him. He's just an arrogant bastard that enjoys me as a little plaything. Isn't that what you used to say to me?' I fold my arms across my chest defensively, as if this can shield me from her expected bitchy retort.

Alice and Brooke lean in, intrigued as to how this is going to go down. If they had the option of popcorn they'd be shamelessly munching on it.

Evelyn sighs, placing her drink on the side table and throwing her sunglasses on. She tilts her head up to the sun, completely unbothered by me, which I find even more maddening.

'Do whatever you want,' she says nonchalantly. 'Just don't come crying to me when it all blows up in your face.'

Ugh, I fucking hate that about Evelyn! *Hello!* Friends are supposed to be there for you when you do stupid stuff. Not to just judge you and say *I told you so*. I have my mother for that.

'Whatever,' I snort.

Yeah, good come-back Erica. Oh, good Lord, I really wish I was better in the moment. I bet I'll have loads of come-backs in an hour or so.

'Anyway,' I turn back to the girls. 'Let's go get ready.'

Chapter 3

Erica

Two hours later we're all done up to the nines. I look into the full-length mirror in mine and Brooke's hotel room, which has become the unofficial getting ready room, and nod my approval. My blonde highlights have grown out enough so that it can pass as trendy ombre hair. I've tousled it to perfection and I've added a small discreet plait in each side—very boho chic.

I'm wearing my long, navy blue, maxi dress with an embellished sweetheart neckline. It's almost completely backless so I have to go bra-less, but I get a thrill knowing these days I can. Years ago, when he knew me I just had bee stings. I had to wear a bra just to get some kind of shape. Now I have some rocking C-cups and I'm eager to show them off.

I've finished my outfit off with a few bangle bracelets, dangly earrings, and my wedge sandals. I don't want to sound arrogant, but I know I look good.

Not that the others don't. They all look amazing. Evelyn's in a classy, satin, black dress that hugs her hourglass figure beautifully and hangs down to just below her knee. Alice is wearing a royal blue, halter-neck dress with white spots—very rockabilly—while Molly is in a hot pink, lace mini skirt with a satin, flowery blouse. She's so adorable; she could pass for a Barbie doll.

Brooke walks in from the bathroom wearing a bright red, skin-tight dress, showing off almost all of her breasts and barely covering her vagina. She's never one to shy away from showing her body. And why the hell should she? For someone that lives off McDonalds she looks amazing.

We exit the elevator and walk towards the all-inclusive bar in our luxury hotel. Thank heavens for the last minute deal we got otherwise there's no way we'd have been able to afford it. I wonder what Jack does to be able to afford a place like this.

I've never felt so nervous in all my life. My mouth is as dry as the Sahara and my hands are shaking uncontrollably. I try to tell myself to calm down, but it's no use.

This is the first guy I ever loved.

The one that got away.

The one I constantly think about, even though I'd

never admit it to any of my friends.

I spot him before he sees me, my heart jumping up and down in happiness. Calm down, you stupid thing. You're just setting yourself up for disappointment.

Slowly, he turns and sees me. His eyes light up and he smiles lazily. Oh crap, not the lazy smile. My stomach starts bubbling with excitement. That smile used to get me every fucking time and my mind and body remembers.

I grin back, but must misstep. Before I know what's happened, I've stood on the front of my dress. I put my other foot out to steady myself but it only drags the dress down further. Oh crap. I'm going down.

I land face down, my hands only managing to break the fall slightly against the hard marbled floor. My nose still throbs in agony. Fuck, that hurts. I pull my head up, wishing I could just press an ejector button like on one of those aeroplanes. Why do I *always* fall?

Brooke's wetting herself laughing while everyone else offers a helping hand. Jack pushes them aside to offer me his. He must have rushed straight over. *My hero.* I tremble, taking his hand in mine. It's so warm and inviting. I want to press it against my cheek.

'You always knew how to make an entrance.' He grins affectionately.

'Oh my God, I can't believe I did that!' I grimace,

covering my face with my hands so I can try and block out everyone staring at me. From the aching, I'd say my nose is starting to swell at a rapid speed.

He grabs my wrists and attempts to pull them down from my face. 'Eric.' I open my eyes to find his face close to mine. 'Ignore them. It's over. Come have a drink with us.'

'O..okay,' I croak, letting him lead me towards the bar. Blimey, why am I having trouble breathing? Did it suddenly get hard to breathe in here?

The feelings I'm having towards him are already bordering on obsessive. I shouldn't be going anywhere near him. Nothing good can come from this. I force myself to sit down regardless. He smiles to the girls before turning to the barman.

'Can we have some ice please?' he asks him, looking at my face in alarm. Jeez, I really hope it's not swelled too big. My nose is already large enough. 'Just like the first time we met,' he says, placing the given ice into a tea towel and pressing it against my nose.

I think back to our first official meeting at the caravan park. His brother had just knocked me down with his Frisbee so he took me to get some ice on it. I realise now why it's called an ice breaker.

'Shit, are you okay?'

I couldn't believe it was the gorgeous boy from

breakfast looking down at me.

'Err....what happened?' I mumbled. Even my voice sounded weird as I clutched my head.

'My idiot brother hit you with the Frisbee. I'm so sorry. Are you okay?'

I forced myself to sit up. He helped, clutching my arm for support.

'Define okay?' I joked, immediately wincing at the pain of attempting to laugh.

He pulled my fringe back from my forehead, his eyebrows creased in concern.

'I think you need to get some ice on it. Our caravan's all the way by the lake. Come into the clubhouse and we'll see if we can get you some ice.'

'Are you sure?' I mumbled. What a first meeting.

'Of course, It's the least I could do. If you play your cards right I might even buy you an ice lolly.'

I grinned. 'Well how could I refuse that?'

We walked in comfortable silence towards the clubhouse. I tried my best not to cry or act like a baby, but my head was throbbing.

'Where's your caravan then?' he asked as we walked. 'Do you want me to get your mum or anything?'

'Oh, please, no!' I shrieked a bit too quickly. He raised his eyebrows in confusion. 'Sorry, it's just...I think her and my dad are...er...unpacking.' They were having

sex. I had the only parents in the world who still insisted on doing it.

He narrowed his eyebrows at me, the hint of a smirk on his lips. His plump, perfect, pink lips.

'But we're number 39 I think.'

His eyes lit up. 'No way! We're in number 40.'

I was so pleased. I could stalk him as much as I liked.

He took me into the bar and asked the barman for some frozen peas.

'So how old are you?' he asked out of nowhere. A bit random.

'I'm fifteen. What about you?'

He smiled, and it was like the sun had just come out. 'Sixteen. I'm glad I'm not the only teenager here. Everyone else seems to be twelve and under.'

Wait, did he think I was twelve?

He took the frozen peas wrapped in a tea towel from the barman. 'This may hurt a little, okay?'

I nodded. Any excuse to gaze into those beautiful eyes. They were a strange colour. A mix between hazel and green. Almost a grey, but not. Weird, but stunning.

He placed the bag onto the side of my head. I grimaced from the cold sting.

He grinned. 'I told you.' He held it there for a while, staring back into my eyes. I looked down, embarrassed by the intensity. I tried to act normal, but it was like I was breathing too heavily. I tried to slow it down, but then it felt like I might pass out from lack of oxygen.

When I looked back up he was still staring at me, a whole lot of potential trouble behind those eyes. 'So...what ice lolly are you going for?

I quickly attempt to pull myself back into the present day and realise I haven't introduced anyone.

'Oh, these are my girls,' I explain, desperate to escape the intense memories. I smile towards his guys. 'You met Brooke.' She winks cheekily making me laugh. 'And Jack, you'll remember Evelyn.' He nods, biting his lip as he smiles at her.

She smiles tightly at him, warning in her eyes. Holy crap, I wish she wouldn't remember *EVERYTHING!* If I'm fine with this she should be too. Why can't she just support me?

'And this is Molly.' She flicks her short blonde hair behind her and smiles brightly. When I say brightly I mean Molly is so cute and loveable that it's like sun beams actually shine from her eyes. No-one ever meets her and doesn't like her. Although they always seem to be shocked when they find out she's a lesbian. I think they expect all lesbians to be thick necked girls in Doctor Martins with a tattoo on their neck. Idiots.

'And Alice.' She purses her red lips into a tight smile,

her porcelain skin shimmering in the light. I notice Nicholas eyeing up the tattoos on her arms. That might be a match there.

'Nicholas, Tom, Charlie,' Jack says nodding round at his lads. 'Anyway, now that we've got the awkward introductions out of the way...shots?'

'Hell, yeah!' Brooke cheers, calling over the barman.

Jack pulls me slightly away from the others so our bar stools are next to each other.

'So...this is weird, right?' he whispers, running his hand through his hair. Christ on a pogo stick, I want to do that.

I cringe and nod, placing the ice back down on the bar, my face feeling better. 'A little. I mean, what are the odds of us meeting up again?'

'Slim. Definitely slim,' he nods with a mischievous smile. 'I thought I'd never see you again.'

'Me too.' I don't want to tell him I tried to look him up on Facebook one time but didn't know his last name. That's the thing nowadays. You don't even ask for a number, you ask if they're on Facebook.

'So...' he claps his hands together. 'How do we catch up on the last fifteen years?'

Shit, I could do without telling him about Karl. I know it's wrong, but I don't want him to know.

I roll my eyes. 'Let's just skip all that bullshit, shall

we? What we do for a living, what we're up to. Why don't we just do some shots and reminisce?'

'Sounds good to me.' He leans over to the barman. 'More shots please.'

I don't know how it happens but after a few hours of us talking exclusively to each other someone suggests we go to a nearby bar. I'm glad for the change of scenery to be honest. We've gone over how we met and funny things that happened, but we've left out any horny details. That, and the reason why we stopped talking.

As we walk towards the bar I can feel the heat of his hand near mine. It's so close I could just move my finger an inch and touch him. And boy do I want to touch him. I might even want to strip him naked and slowly stroke all of him with a feather duster. Instead I ignore it and smile shyly every time he looks at me.

The resort of Luna Island has remained non-commercialised for years—most people choosing to come to experience the culture and uninterrupted sunshine. I suppose that explains the oldies. Because of that it's only a short walk until we're at the one bar on their small rustic high street.

As soon as we arrive I make a point of getting a cocktail to try to steady my nerves. This place is so random. Painted purple, with red leather stools, and a large wooden dance floor, it could pass more as a run-down strip club than a bar.

Jack's phone flashes up with an *'Amber'* calling. It vibrates along the sticky wooden bar. He quickly dismisses it. A flush of jealously comes over me, my fists clenching.

Is that his girlfriend? Is that the same Amber "friend" that I was jealous of all those years ago? How the hell can he be flirting with me when he's got a girlfriend back home? Is he even flirting? Is he just being friendly and because of my obsession I'm reading way too much into it?

Then I realise what a massive hypocrite I am. Even if Amber is his girlfriend, here I am flirting away without a second thought of Karl. I need to stay away from him. He makes me stupid.

Hypnotize by The Notorious B.I.G. starts blasting out of the speakers. Damn, I love this song! I hit the dance floor with the girls. I want to show him that I'm not going to be fawning all over him during this holiday. Which, you know, I kind of want to do.

I'm conscious of him watching me the entire time so I put a bit more of a sashay into my steps as Brooke dances up against me. Bless her, she dances like a crack-whore stripper desperate for her next hit.

When a group of local creeps come over and start being letchy with us, instead of ignoring them I chat back. I know it's pathetic, but I want to make him jealous. I want to make him so bloody jealous it pains him not to be able to touch me. I want to make him want me even half as much as I want him. I couldn't tell you the amount of times I fantasized about seeing him in this exact situation, when I'm looking this good and showing him what he missed out on by being a dick.

The creeps only speak Spanish so I can't make out what they're saying, but I notice some key words like "sexy" and "apartment". *Yeah, I don't think so buddy.* I grab Brooke and make my way back over to the boys.

I smile at Jack, but he seems weird. On closer inspection, his eyes are glassy and his grin lopsided. He's totally bloody shit faced. Crap. That wasn't my plan at all. Since when did he become such a lightweight?

'Erica,' he slurs when he sees me. 'You're so beautiful.'

My mouth drops open. Wow. He's never said anything that nice to me before. Brooke raises her eyebrows at me in amusement.

'Thanks,' I fake gush. 'You know, I totally wash my face twice a day. It's my secret.' I laugh at my own joke. *Maybe I'm a little drunk too.*

He cracks up, his laugh like bubbling chocolate to my

ear drums.

'And you're so fucking *funny*. You were always so funny.'

Charlie looks at me with raised eyebrows. He pats Jack on the back. 'Alright champ. I think it's time we got you home. Don't you?'

'I'm fwine here,' he slurs. He looks up to me with smitten eyes. 'Wherever Erica is, that's where I want to be.' He takes my hand in his. Crap, it's warm. I imagine what it feels like stroking itself lazily over my body. Then he belches loudly. Wow. *Romantic.*

He won't let go of my hand. Charlie rolls his eyes at me. 'Do you mind helping me get him home?'

'It's fine,' I chuckle, glad to still have his hand in mine.

We arrange for the others to make their way back too. I try to guide Jack, but he drops my hand and quickly swings his arm around my shoulders. I try not to snuggle into him and ask what aftershave he's wearing. That would look desperate.

He's so drunk he's walking in zig-zags, dragging me all over the street, which is pretty dangerous in a place like this. Even at 2am the road is packed with drivers with no regard for safety. He's like a sleepy toddler. Keeping him out of the way of cars is a mission in itself.

'Why didn't we work out, Erica? Huh? I always

wondered.'

Shit. Him bringing up this stuff to me when drunk is not the ideal scenario. It's not like we can have a proper chat now. And even if we did, he's bound to have forgotten everything by the morning.

'The distance was probably a problem,' I deadpan as I try to steer him out of the road and back onto the pavement.

'But apart from that.'

'I really don't think now's the time to discuss this.'

Thankfully, we're already almost back at our hotel. We head up in the lift and Charlie leads me towards their hotel room. It turns out it's only down the corridor from ours. How convenient. Or worrying. Whichever way you look at it.

Charlie opens the door. Together, we help to throw Jack onto his already messy, single bed. He's asleep in an instant, a light snore falling from his lips. I look at his peaceful sleeping form. He's so hot. Even as a sleepy drunk.

'Apparently, our lot are meeting in the lobby for another drink,' Charlie says while getting some money out of his drawer.

'Okay. I'll just be a minute.'

I wait until Charlie's heading for the door and then try to assess whether Jacks a danger to himself. I decide to loosen his belt. I heard something about drunk people not being restricted or something.

He stirs slightly. 'Oooh, cheeky!' he giggles. I've never heard him giggle. It makes me ridiculously happy.

I roll my eyes and begrudgingly leave him. I want nothing more than to snuggle up next to him in that bed. His eyes are closed but it doesn't stop me from blowing a kiss when Charlie isn't looking.

'So, you fancy meeting back up with the rest of them?' Charlie asks with a mischievous glint in his eye.

'Yeah, why not,' I shrug.

Chapter 4

Erica

In truth, I just want to go to bed and replay the whole evening in my head, dissecting every stolen glance until I feel l know what's going on. But I refuse to let myself do that. I came on this holiday to have fun and let loose, and damn it, that's what I'm going to do.

We go back into the lobby to find our friends squashed around one table, all looking slightly pissed. Alice is looking cosy with Nicholas, asking about all his tattoos. All the other tables and chairs have been packed away, only dim lights left on. I really need to catch up with them. I feel like I've sobered up too much. I take Brooke's shot and down it.

'What have I missed?'

Molly giggles, pointing behind me. 'Evelyn's at the bar chatting up the barman.'

Last time I looked at the barman he was an

overweight local man. I look over and to my relief some hottie has come on shift. Thank the Lord I don't have to commit her to the nearest mental hospital.

'We were just about to play truth or dare,' Brooke tells me, sitting on Tom's lap. They got cosy pretty quickly. I knew those two would get on. I'd say they're a perfect match, both total tarts.

'Yeah, sit down, twiglet,' Tom says with a cheeky smile. 'I've got some questions for you.'

Twiglet? I'm not that bloody skinny.

'Uh-oh,' I wince, reluctantly sitting down on the bamboo chair.

Molly and Alice start giggling with Charlie over some joke he's telling. Bless him, he might have put on weight but he's still the loveliest guy in the world. Not that I reckon Alice fancies him. Charlie's looking at Molly like a little lost puppy. Uh-oh. Someone needs to tell him she's not into guys.

'Ok,' Tom says eyeing me suggestively. 'Truth or dare?'

Oh, for fucks sakes, I knew he'd pick on me immediately. I hate dares. I'd probably be dared to streak through the hotel naked and I am NOT down with that.

I sigh. 'Truth.'

'Okay.' His eyes grow devilish and dark. I gulp, re-arranging myself on my chair. 'What really happened with you and Jack all those years ago?'

My stomach churns, my pulse quickening. Shit. Charlie stops his joke and listens in.

'What do you mean?' I shrug, avoiding eye contact. Instead I pretend to inspect my thumb nail.

'I mean what happened? Jack's refusing to tell us, and he has Charlie sworn to secrecy. But I'm not blind. You guys were together, right?'

'Err...' I twist my hands in my lap. 'Sort of.'

'Come on,' Nicholas nods, leaning in. 'I wanna hear too.'

'It's...complicated.' What the hell am I supposed to say anyway? Yeah, I was obsessed with him and then he broke my heart.

'Yeah, leave her alone,' Charlie chimes in. 'It's nobody's business.' I knew I liked him.

Tom puts his palms up in defence. 'Hey, that's fine. But that means you have to do a dare.'

Oh, Fuck.

'Fine,' I snap. 'But I'm not running naked around the hotel.' Best to cover myself.

'You have to...' I watch as his mind wanders off. What is this sadistic bastard going to suggest?

'Get off with Tom,' Nicholas interrupts.

My stomach drops. Get off with Tom? Where the hell did that come from? Tom and Brooke both squirm uncomfortably, trying not to look at each other. Well hasn't this fucked up their laughing little faces. Why on earth would Nicholas want us to kiss?

'Well, I suppose a dare's a dare,' Tom smirks. 'Come here, twiglet.' He unwraps his arm from Brooke and holds both armsout to me dramatically.

I can't snog him. I have a boyfriend. Not that I can tell him that without it getting back to Jack. And God help me, I really don't want that to happen. Jesus, I'm a terrible person.

I look to Brooke. It's pretty hard for her not to feel dejected right now and I need her permission that it's okay. If she seriously likes this guy I don't want to mess anything up for her. She discreetly nods. So discreetly no-one else would know it even existed.

'Fine.' I snap, standing up and walking over to him. I take a deep breath.

This is beyond awkward. Brooke is still sitting on his lap for heaven's sake.

He takes my face in his hands and pulls me so close that I can smell the lager on his breath. Eww. My gaze travels up from his lips to his mesmerising, green eyes. He wiggles his eyebrows comically which makes me giggle. Then he pulls me in, crushing his plump lips onto mine. His tongue forces itself past my pursed lips and then he's caressing my tongue with it. My jaw goes slack as I allow myself to enjoy it for a second.

Then I smash back into reality. I don't even like this guy. I pull back sharpish. Everyone's staring at me. My cheeks are practically puce.

I make my way back to my seat in an awkward silence.

'Well, this is uncomfortable,' Charlie chuckles, attempting and failing to break the atmosphere.

'Right, my turn,' I announce, locking my steely eyes with Tom. Payback time. 'Truth or dare, Tom?'

'Dare,' he nods, leaning back in his chair. He pulls Brooke back firmly onto his lap, looking ever so confident. Arrogant arse.

'Strip off and run around this whole hotel screaming *I have crabs*!'

He snorts in disbelief. 'I don't think so. I'll *obviously* change it to truth.'

'Even better,' I smile evilly. 'If Brooke sleeps with you, will you be onto your next victim tomorrow?'

Brooke glares at me. She hates when I ruin her fun. She flicks her hair behind her shoulders and turns to face him, her lips quirked in amusement. 'Well, answer the girl.'

He stretches dramatically, pretending to check his watch. 'Is that the time? I think I'm gonna go to bed.'

'Fuck off,' Nicholas laughs. 'Tell the truth.'

'Yeah,' Brooke says, glaring at him in warning. 'I'm a big girl.'

He visibly squirms in his seat before turning to her. 'Look babe, I'm just not a one-woman kind of guy.'

She throws back her head cackling. 'Luckily for you, I'm not a one-man kind of girl.'

She plunges her tongue in his mouth and before you know it they're making their excuses and heading off to bed together. I hope not to our room. I could do without a night of plugging my ears. It wouldn't be the first time.

Jack

I wake up to my phone beeping. I grab it, wiping the sleep out of my eyes, to see that it's Tom.

'Breakfast in ten minutes.'

God, that bastard is always hungry.

I've also got a missed call from Amber and a voicemail saying nothing is wrong, just checking you got there safely.

Charlie is snoring away on the bed next to me. He really needs to see a doctor about that. It's so loud I'm half expecting all the fish in the sea to beach themselves in protest.

'Charlie.' I lean over and punch him in the arm.

'Charlie!'

He snorts, waking up with a cough. 'What's wrong?' he panics, looking round as if half expecting the hotel to be on fire.

'Nothing. Just that we should get up for breakfast.'

He rolls over, closing his eyes again. 'I bet you're starving after all you put away last night.'

Last night? I try to trace my mind back. Then it comes shooting back to me, cringeworthy memories smacking me in the face. Getting shit-faced drunk. Oh, fuck, what an impression I must have made on Erica.

I can remember her dancing with the girls and feeling insanely jealous and territorial when those other guys were checking her out. Those fuckers, only after one thing. I suppose I drank to control my rage or jealousy, if you want to put it that way.

I try desperately to remember anything after that but it's all a bit hazy. Shit, did Erica put me to bed?

'Did I make a dick out of myself?' I ask quietly, not really wanting to know the answer. I stare up at the ceiling, unable to watch his reaction.

He chuckles. 'You were all over Erica, telling her how beautiful she is.'

I smack my hands over my eyes. 'Fuck!'

'Don't worry,' a voice tells me. I look to the end of my bed and find Nicholas, his hair in disarray. 'As far as

I could tell you didn't confess your undying love for her.'

I snort. 'Well, that's something I suppose.' I rub my hand over my face, as if I can scrub away the embarrassment. 'What the fuck are you doing in here anyway?'

Nicholas rolls his eyes. 'Tom decided to fuck Brooke all night. I tried to sleep in the hallway I was so knackered, but the sounds out of their mouths.' He shudders. 'It was some freaky shit.'

I laugh, but look to Charlie, wanting him to tell me more about my behaviour last night.

He smiles, as if reading my mind. 'You were pretty annoying,' he admits with a grimace. 'She basically had to carry you home and help me put you to bed.'

Carry me home? How bloody strong is she?

'Great. So, the short answer is yes; I did make a dick out of myself.'

What is it about that girl that brings out the worst in me?

Chapter 5

Erica

Scrambled or fried? I look down at the breakfast buffet trying to work out what is supposed to be what. The scrambled look completely dried up and hard. Gross. The fried look like someone had started to make them scrambled and then remembered they were supposed to be fried. Maybe I should have cereal.

'Alright, Eric?'

I immediately flush at the sound of his voice and its proximity to my ear. I turn around to see him standing there in loose swimming shorts which hang from his lean hips and a white t-shirt. The t-shirt isn't tight, but it still clings to just the right places, showing off his lean physique and biceps. It really should be illegal for anyone to be that good looking, especially at this time in the morning.

Something splatters on the floor at my feet. I look

down to see a still intact fried egg on the floor. Jesus, I must have picked it up. My hand's got a spatula in it. What the fuck is happening where I can't remember picking up eggs? My brain just doesn't work properly around him.

I stoop down to pick it up, glad that I can hide my flushing face from his. Only he stoops down to help at the same time. We both scramble (ha ha, get it) to pick it up, only it's a slippery fucker. I wish he'd stop trying to help me. He's just pushing it further away. I can feel myself sweating now. We're drawing a small crowd, desperate to find out what the hell has happened.

'Just let me get it,' I snap, swatting the egg myself.

I swat it too hard, the egg breaking open, yolk oozing everywhere. Well fuck a duck, I've screwed this right up!

I look up to him in panic, my heart thumping so hard I'm sure it's going to jump out of my chest and run away. He stares back aghast for a second, but it's quickly replaced with a humour filled smile. Fuck, he's beautiful.

'Quick.' He grabs my hand and pulls me up, dragging me out of the canteen area before I even have a chance to say *"eggs over easy"*.

He stops when we're at reception and turns to me, eyebrows furrowed.

'Are you okay?' he asks, trying to keep a straight face, the hint of a smirk playing on his lips.

I can't look at that mischievous face any longer. Hysterical laughter bubbles up inside me until I combust into loud cackles. He joins in and within seconds we're both doubled over crying and clutching our stomachs.

'Trust you,' he sniggers with an affectionate smile. 'That could seriously only happen to you.'

'Shut up.' I push him in a totally juvenile manner. It would appear I'm reverting to my teenage self around him.

'Anyway,' he tries to straighten himself up, his expression quickly turning sombre. 'I wanted to apologise for last night. The boys said I was pretty shit-faced and I'm sure I made a dick out of myself.' He scratches the back of his neck, as if worried about what he might have said.

I smile knowingly, torturing him for a second.

'You were fine really,' I admit, hating seeing the worry on those beautiful features. I didn't want to be the cause of unnecessary wrinkles.

He frowns, chewing his bottom lip. 'You're sure?'

'Yeah,' I nod, trying not to get distracted by the lip biting. Why the hell does he insist on teasing me? I shake my head, to try to gather my thoughts. 'Why? What were you worried you'd said?'

Does he have some idea? Does he actually remember calling me beautiful, but not want to admit it?

'Oh...nothing. Nothing at all. Anyway, let's go to the pool.'

I've just about calmed down by the time we're settled around the pool. Not that the sudden smacking of heat has done anything to calm my flushed self down. Fuck, it's hot. You feel it more after leaving the air conditioned lobby.

All the loungers were taken by some crazy bastards that clearly got up at the crack of dawn, so instead of being on one of the luxury loungers, we've taken up residence on the grass. Our towels are spread out and we even wedged a huge umbrella into the grass for some shade. It's not so bad.

'Here,' Jack says, handing me a cereal bar. 'I figured after that fiasco you'd still be hungry.'

Sweet baby Jesus, he's perfect. Give me a man who feeds me and I'll fall in love quickly.

'Thanks,' I all but swoon. Jeez, pull yourself together Erica. It's a cereal bar, not an engagement ring.

Jack takes his t-shirt off so I get to see that torso. Fuck me, has it improved. He must be one of those boring gym bastards at home because he is built perfectly. Not like a gladiator though, gross veins protruding. Just perfect lean muscles going down to his V line.

'Right,' Jack says, clapping his hands together and pulling me from my perving. 'Who's up for a swim?'

He looks bloody gorgeous in those black swimming shorts. He now has a short sleeve tattoo on the top of his left arm. They're all kinds of images meshed together, but the only thing I can make out properly is a vintage looking clock. I don't want to be caught staring at his arm.

'Me!' Brooke sings back, springing up to standing and re-tying her bikini top. She told me this morning in great detail how she slept with Tom last night. Apparently he has the stamina of a horse and did three rounds with our acrobatic and equally energetic Brooke. Poor Nicholas apparently was so horrified he bunked in with Jack and Charlie.

It doesn't seem to have fazed her at all. When she saw Tom she just blew him a cheeky kiss and then carried on as normal, as if they didn't exchange bodily fluids just a few hours before.

'Yeah, me too,' Molly adds. Trust her. She's always so bloody cheery. She looks doubly adorable today in her cherry print bikini.

'Great,' he cheers.

'I'm in too,' Alice says begrudgingly. 'It's too bloody hot here.' I don't even know why she agreed to come. She wears factor 50 so she can keep her skin as milky as possible. Apparently, it works for her rockabilly look. I often wonder what she'd look like with boring coloured hair and no tattoos. Probably completely unrecognisable.

'What about you Eric?' he asks leaning over me so I'm shadowed from the sun. Shit, he's sexy. The urge to stick my tongue out and lick his leg is strong.

I remember how we used to splash around in the pool together, normally ending with him trying to dunk me under the water. Short of him kicking me in the vagina, I'm guessing it was his way of telling me he fancied me. I just wish every time I came back up I didn't have smudged mascara and bogies hanging out of my nose.

'Nah. I think I'm gonna read my book.' *And fantasize about having sex with you.*

A playful smirk twitches his lips as he stares at my Kindle. 'At least it's the right way round this time.'

I can't help but smile at the memory. I can't believe he remembered that. All those years ago, he caught me pretending to read a book while ogling him, but it was completely upside down. I had *no game* back then.

'Just leave the poor girl alone,' Tom snaps. 'We'll take good care of her.' His eyes squint, lit with an inner twinkle of mischief. I blush like a teenager. I stand corrected; I *still* have zero game.

Jack's face falls. 'That's what I'm worried about,' he says under his breath, just loud enough for us to hear.

He walks away and dives into the pool, still as effortless as if he were sixteen. Shit the bed, he's athletic. I have to fight the urge to lower my sunglasses and shout *'bow chicka wow wow.'*

'So, then,' Charlie says, putting his phone away.

Oh, crap, is he going to ask me about Molly? I really don't fancy being the one to tell him, but if he asks I won't lie.

'What happened with you and Jack?

Oh, G, it's worse. Info on us. I really can't be doing with a grilling right now.

'Huh?' I say, pretending to be really into my book.

'Yeah,' Tom grins, lowering his sunglasses. 'Me and Nic didn't know Jack back then. What the hell went down all those years ago to cause so much sexual tension?

'Sexual tension?' I blurt with a snort. *Is it noticeable?* 'We're just friends.'

'Okay,' they all laugh, as if I'm some hilarious stand up comic. I put the book up closer to my face in an attempt to hide the blushes firing up my cheeks.

Then I remember the missed call from Amber. This could be my opportunity to find out a bit about her. Act like I know already.

'He has a girlfriend anyway,' I state, as if he's told me himself.

Tom lowers his glasses to reveal eyes burning with

confusion. 'Err, no he doesn't.'

'Really? But I thought...?' He had a missed call from her. A friend wouldn't bother calling someone so far away, right? And can guys ever really be friends with girls?

'Nah,' Nicholas confirms with a firm shake of his head. 'He hasn't dated seriously since.'

'Since?' I frown. 'Since what?'

'Guys!' Charlie interrupts, with a warning glare.

What the hell is he trying to keep hidden? What is going on here? Since *what?*

'He just prefers to play the field,' Tom comments with a wink, 'just like me.'

Well what the hell is that all about? So, Amber *isn't* his girlfriend? Perhaps just a girl toy he hooks up with occasionally? I don't know whether I feel better or worse about that. And I really shouldn't care. *I'm* the one with a boyfriend. I really have to deal with Karl at some point.

'Do you guys want a drink?' I ask, desperately trying to get away from this line of conversation.

'You're eager to change the subject,' Nicholas says, showing a rare smile. Wow, when he does smile he's stunning. He has the most perfect set of teeth.

Tom chuckles. 'Are you trying to suss out if you can get back into Jack's pants?'

I stand up, choosing to ignore him completely.

Fucking hell, he's an arse. 'Beer? Cocktail?'

'Go on then.' They all agree on beers even though it's only 11am. I suppose it's 5pm somewhere.

I have to walk past the swimming pool the others are in to get to the outdoor bar. I pull my shoulders back and walk as slowly as I can around it. I need to concentrate on not falling in. I attempt a sashay, but for all I know I could look constipated. I don't do sexy well.

I can see them in my peripheral vision splashing each other. Is Brooke flirting with him? Please don't tell me now she's bedded Tom she's setting her sights on Jack. I might have to bitch slap her. But then I've told the girls I'm only interested in him as a friend. Still, I'd like to think that as my friend she can read between the lines. Is that too much to ask? I don't think so.

I get the beers from the young barman, who seems to be ogling my boobs, and walk back around the pool. It really is stunning here; one huge main pool surrounded by the most luxurious looking brown marble tiles. You can see the white sandy beach from here, the sea breeze giving us some rest from the blazing sun.

Jack pulls me from my thoughts, jumping out so he's blocking my path, a dripping wet Adonis. My mouth falls open of its own accord. I force myself to keep my tongue in my mouth.

'Sure you don't want to come in for a play, Eric?' he

asks, his eyes dancing with danger. Oh lordy, it's tempting. What I really want to do is lick him dry and massage suntan lotion into his muscles, but I get a feeling I'd come across a *bit* desperate.

'No thanks. *Eric-A* is fine, thanks.' I smile, pleased at my playing hard to get. Now to just continue for the rest of the holiday and I'll be grand.

He smirks at me, licking his lips. Fuck balls, how I want to lick them myself.

'You know I could just push you in, right?' He taunts.

I gasp, a thrill of excitement going through me and ending up in my lady parts.

'I thought you'd grown up since I last met you.' I counter, the beers still in my hand. I move around him to take them to the boys, praying to God he doesn't decide to throw me in anyway. Knowing my luck, I'd smash my head on the side, turn the pool red and end up needing stitches.

He lets me past. I'm better leaving him to flirt with Brooke. If he wants her I'm not going to get in his way. Especially if he's the love-them-and-leave-them sort like his mates say.

'You're the best, Erica,' Charlie calls when he sees me with the beers.

Tom takes his. 'Yeah and not a bad kisser, either.' He winks at me, his green eyes lit up in amusement.

I grimace, my cheeks burning up. ‘Let’s never talk about that again, okay?’

He chuckles to himself. ‘I’ve never had any complaints before!’

I bet he hasn’t; man-whore like him.

Once I’ve settled myself back down on my towel, I get my kindle back out and start to read. Anything to stop my cheeks turning tomato red. Imagine Tom bringing up the kiss like that. How mortifying!

Plus, I could really do with Jack not finding out. I don’t want him to think I’m some hussy. He was always jealous when we were younger and I’m not sure if that’s something you outgrow.

Jack

I can’t bear knowing she’s over there with the lads while I’m here in the pool, trying to avoid the dirty looks Evelyn’s shooting my way. I’m sure Erica was aware of me as she walked away with the beers for them. She’s never been good at hiding those blushes. I don’t even think of myself as the jealous type, but fuck me, if I don’t want to pound them in the head for even daring to look at her in her tie-dye bikini.

Knowing Tom, he’ll already be trying it on with her.

I hope she sees past his bullshit. More than that I hope she only has eyes for me. Yeah, that might sound fucking arrogant, but I remember how we were all those years ago. We were obsessed with each other. Surely feelings like that don't just go away? They clearly haven't for me.

I just have to think of an excuse to talk to her. Before I come up with any sort of solid plan I'm lifting myself out of the pool and walking towards her. I block her sun, throwing her into my shade. She looks up just as water starts dripping from my chest onto her stomach. She jumps in shock. It makes my dick twitch in my shorts. *Don't get a boner here.* These swim shorts are completely unforgiving.

She looks back down at her Kindle, as if completely uninterested. I know better though. I can make out the slightest pink in her cheeks and the smile playing on the edges of her lips.

I sit down on the edge of her towel and shake my hair around, flicking water on both her and her Kindle. That should get her attention.

'Careful!' she shrieks.

Fuck, her nipples are hard. They're easy to make out in that flimsy bikini. I try my hardest not to stare, but it's tough. I've never been a big tit man, but fuck if Erica's aren't perfect. It's true what they say, patience is a virtue. Are they erect from the water or is she turned on? Is she reading one of those mummy porn books?

'What's in this book that's so good?' I grab her Kindle and scan over the page. I press the top corner to see what it is, half expecting to see something like Erotic Plumbers, but instead it's some teenager book.

'No way! You're reading Twilight?' I can't help but openly scoff. 'I thought that shit was for teenagers?'

Her cheeks turn even pinker. She snatches it back, turning away from me.

'Well, maybe I'm reminiscing about being a teenager again.'

Shit, does she mean because I remind her of being a teenager? Is she wanting to relive her youth because of bumping into me? Fuck, I hope so.

Fuck, I need her in that pool with me. I need an excuse to touch her.

'You should be in the pool with us. Come on, we're gonna have a volleyball game.'

'Volleyball?' Charlie hollers, his eyes lighting up excitedly. 'That shit is my game!' He goes running off towards the pool. He's such a geek.

I turn to Erica. We lock eyes, both clearly thinking the same thing. We burst out laughing hysterically. I love when she laughs. She has the cutest little chuckle.

'Knowing you, you'd probably try to drown me again,' she says, seeming genuinely scared. She's adorable. Of course I'm going to dunk her.

God, doesn't she know that I'm just looking for an excuse to feel her skin against mine? Surely everyone knows by now that when a boy drowns a girl in a pool it's because he fancies her?

'What if I pinkie swore?' I hold up my little finger and pout out my lower lip. She always used to melt when I'd do that.

'Ugh, fine,' she relents, faking indifference. I still got it.

I watch as she lowers herself into the pool, smiling, as if surprised at the warmth of it.

Do not get a boner. Do not get a boner.

I lower myself in. I catch her watching my stomach muscles contracting. I grin; yeah, she wants this.

She swims over to the others, attempting to ignore me. I swim quickly behind her like a pussy whipped little bitch.

'So, shall we do boys against girls?' Molly asks innocently, all cute wide eyes. She's the sweetest.

'Whatever,' Tom shrugs, 'let's just get started.' He launches the ball over the net and Brooke immediately bounces it back to him, her tits almost escaping out of her bikini top.

He shoots it back to our side. Erica's ass is suddenly backing up into my dick. Fuck. I wince my eyes shut in effort, but it's no use. I get a semi.

She looks behind her shoulder at me. I quickly attempt to get the ball so I don't have to look at her. I manage to hit it back over to Brooke who smashes it back.

Erica tries to leap into the air for it, but I'm not letting her win. I grab her around the waist and throw her to the right, inadvertently dunking her under the water.

She splutters, spitting out water. 'What the fuck, Jack?' she gasps, her eyes wide with innocent betrayal.

I can't help but grin. 'Hey, I'm just trying to play the game.'

She clenches her jaw, a new steely determination in her eyes. 'Oh, it's on now.'

The ball is bounced towards us again and this time she's backing up into me deliberately, swaying her arse suggestively against my now completely hard dick.

'Fuck,' I hiss, losing concentration. She gets to hit the ball.

The next time it comes back she pushes her arse back again. Shit, she's completely playing me.

I practically growl. 'Two can play that game you know,' I whisper into her ear.

I press my erection against her arse cheeks. Fuck! This game just took on a whole other level. I want her to look back, acknowledge me somehow, but she doesn't. Instead she freezes in place, her breathing laboured. Hell, it feels good.

Just when I think she might freak out, she instead presses her butt back against me greedily. Oh yeah! That's it Erica. I take hold of her hips and adjust so my dick is pressed against her pussy. One little slip of those flimsy bikini bottoms to the side and I could be inside her in seconds.

She looks around at the others, probably wondering if it's obvious, but everyone seems none the wiser. This is awful. If I carry on like this for much longer I'm going to come in my swim shorts like some horny fourteen year old.

'Erm...I think I left my travel iron on,' she suddenly says out of nowhere, not particularly to anyone.

What the fuck? She's going to suddenly stop now? Just when it's getting hot and heavy. I was expecting an invite back to her hotel room, not her leaving me with blue balls.

She swims to the edge, get outs, grabs her towel and flees as quickly as she can.

Chapter 6

Erica

I still can't believe I let that happen. Yes, of course I wanted it to, but that doesn't mean that it's right. I've already had three texts from Evelyn asking where I sneaked off to. She *knows,* I know she does. Evelyn knows everything. She's like one of those mums with eyes in the back of her head.

But fuck me, when I think of his thick erection pressing into my arse it's hard to feel sorry. It's impossible not to feel turned on and like I want to go to bed just so that I can dream of him touching me for real. I know he treated me badly in the past, but what's wrong with a bit of a holiday romance?

You have a boyfriend. Oh, shut up sensible side of my brain.

The door to the apartment opens. I brace myself, half expecting Evelyn to come running in to smack some sense into me. I smile when I see Brooke walking in. Followed by Evelyn. Shit. Just when I thought I was safe. She looks mad.

'Why the hell did you run off?' she shrieks, coming straight for me.

'Did I?' I ask vaguely, avoiding her enquiring eyes. 'I just fancied a bit of time out of the sun.'

'Bullshit,' Brooke cackles. 'You just wanted to come up here so you could touch yourself while thinking of Jack.' She lifts an eyebrow comically.

'Brooke!' I screech, slapping her on the shoulder.

'Oh please,' she laughs, rolling her eyes. 'Like we didn't all see you rubbing against each other like a pair of horny kittens.'

Oh my God, they saw? My cheeks fire up. This is mortifying. If they saw, did everyone?

'I really can't believe you,' Evelyn says, on a sigh. 'You're falling into the same pattern as when you were bloody fifteen! How the hell do you see this ending well? He still lives in Peterborough.'

I roll my eyes. *Thanks for stating the obvious.*

'That's not even that far away,' I shrug, pretending to inspect my toe nails.

Her face turns murderous. 'Please don't tell me you've got some ridiculous fantasy in your head that he's going to fall in love with you.'

Ouch. That hurt more than it should have.

'Of course I haven't.' I fold my arms over my chest. 'I just think you're so against us.'

'Of course I am! I had to clear up the mess he left last time.'

'How bad was she?' Brooke asks, clearly intrigued as she rubs in some aftersun.

I glare at Evelyn, hoping she plays it down.

'She was bloody broken.' Jeez, always with the drama! 'I've never seen a person cry that much in my whole life. And even when she stopped and said she was over it, you could still see she wasn't.' She locks eyes with me, a sympathetic smile on her lips. 'It's like the lights in her eyes went out and she was just going through the motions.'

'Shit,' Brooke gasps, grimacing at me.

I still remember it like it only happened yesterday, the pain fresh in my heart. After the holiday we chatted every day on the phone for three months. My Mum invited him and his family up for her 40th birthday so we finally had a chance to see each other again. He came up with Charlie. We snuck off from the party and headed back to the hotel room they were sharing with his younger brother.

We started making out, got naked, but I was so bloody nervous. It showed when he tried to finger me and

I was like a bloody vice. I could tell he was frustrated which just made it worse. It had to happen that day. There was so much pressure on it. His brother walking in eventually stopped everything anyway.

When he'd gone back I'd texted him and said I was sorry I was so nervous. Asked if he thought we'd have another chance to try to have sex again.

I still remember his devastating text. *'I couldn't even get my finger up there. What makes you think I'll ever be able to fuck you?'*

It still to this day is single-handedly the worst and most severe text I've received and I've had some humdingers. I think it's because he was my first love. That's the only way to explain the hurt. I didn't text back and neither did he. He tried to call once a few days later but I didn't answer, too embarrassed. And that was it. The end of our love affair.

Yet that didn't stop me thinking about him, blaming myself for being too scared and timid. Wishing I'd never asked him the question in the first place. We were so happy and I ruined it. I should have answered his call, heard him out. But my pride outweighed my heart.

'It wasn't that bad,' I huff, rolling my eyes. Everyone cries over their first love.

'It was,' Evelyn snaps, in her typical know it all way. 'You need to stay away from him. No good can come from you two hooking up. No good.'

'I told you there's nothing going on anyway, so just stop your whinging.'

She huffs. 'I'm sorry that I have to be the sensible one all the time, but I don't want you getting hurt again. Plus, there's Karl to think about.'

Fuck, I keep forgetting about him. How can I be rubbing up against someone's erection and still have a boyfriend at home? I'm going to hell.

'Yes Mum,' I snarl with an eye roll. The worst thing is I know she's right about Karl. I can't keep ignoring it. 'I'm going to send him an email and tell him it's over.'

'That's brave,' Evelyn snorts sarcastically.

'Yeah, well I know I'm a wimp, but I have to end it now while I'm sure. Now can you please leave me alone to nap in peace?'

Just looking at her judgy face is pissing me off right now.

She smiles sadly, placing her hand on my shoulder. 'Okay. Have a good sleep babe.' Now I feel bad. She only cares.

'See you later buzzkill,' Brooke laughs, as she shows her out. The minute the door is shut Brooke runs on over to me, diving onto my bed. 'You're not gonna listen to that bore off, are you?'

'Brooke! Don't be mean.' She's always saying

Evelyn's too reserved.

'Come on! I don't care how much you cried back then, you were sixteen for fuck's sake. You probably cried when Marissa died in the OC too.'

'Oh my god, don't even talk about that,' I pretend sob. But seriously, I cried like a baby! Why did they have to kill her off? She was my favourite.

'You're a grown ass woman now and if you want to fuck him, I say fuck him.' She's so matter of fact about stuff like this. It makes me wonder why she's never dreamed of falling in love. Or even hanging onto a guy for longer than a week.

'Your answer is always to fuck, regardless of the question!' I screech with a giggle.

'Which is why I have such a fun and fulfilling life. Maybe you should take my advice more.' She wiggles her eyebrows.

'I'm not going to fuck Jack,' I state as confidently as I can. He doesn't deserve me. Not after denting my confidence so badly all those years ago. I need to hang onto that hurt and use it against him as my protection.

'Why not?' she asks with a shrug. 'He's obviously hot for you.'

'Do you think?' I ask, trying to hide my smile. I mean, I know the guy had a boner pressed against me, but after everything that happened I feel like I need the reassurance.

'Duh, you dumbass! And you've done it before, why not do it again? At least this time you're not going to fall for him. You know it's just a holiday fling.'

'The thing is...we never really did *it*.'

'What?' She seems horrified. 'I thought you lost your V card to him?'

I think back to the awkwardness of it all. 'It's a long embarrassing story that I really don't want to have to re-live.'

'Whatever. All the better. Show him how good in bed you are.'

'I could be crap for all you know!' I laugh, thinking back to past lovers. I suppose I've never had any complaints. But most guys are just pleased to get their dicks wet, right?

'Please, bitch,' she scoffs, 'I've seen you dance. Those hips don't lie.'

I chuckle loudly. This is why I need Brooke in my life. She totally counter balances Evelyn's seriousness. They're like the angel and the devil on my shoulder.

'Only you could say that! What about Evelyn?'

She winks. 'What she doesn't know won't hurt her.'

She thinks I should lie and do it all secretly? Crap, this is enough to give me a headache.

'How can you just land this all on me right before my

nap?'

'Sorry,' she grimaces, not looking that apologetic at all. 'Sleep well spider monkey and have some sexy dreams about lover boy.'

Chapter 7

Karl,

I know this is a really shitty thing to do, but I think we need to talk. I don't think this relationship is going anywhere. I so appreciate how you've supported me, but you deserve someone who deserves you. We're better off as friends.

Erica x

I know it's the total wimps way out, but I just know that if I call him I'll change my mind the minute I hear his soothing voice. I'll remember how well he's treated me and how he doesn't deserve this. At least this way it's done.

Tonight we've all signed up for an excursion into the mountains to see how the local people live. I grab my bag and take a deep breath. Brooke went to curl Alice's hair so I've got no-one to confide in about how terrible I feel. You can do this Erica. The worst part is over now.

I open the door and almost smash my face into Jack's chest. He has his fist up, as if he was about to knock.

'Jack!' I shout, far too loudly.

He smiles, his eyes amused at my high pitched voice. 'Hi Eric. Thought I'd walk you to the bus.'

'Great!' I can't stop my voice from being shrill. I sound like a dog's squeaky toy.

He grabs my hand and walks forward, practically dragging me behind him. He's holding my hand? What the hell is going on here?

'So...are we going to talk about what we did earlier?' he asks. I can't read his face from back here. Without seeing him there's no way to tell from his tone whether he regrets it or enjoyed it.

'Err...I'd prefer not to,' I admit sheepishly, my cheeks burning.

'How did I know?' he chuckles, still not looking back.

We're almost at the bus now, our crowd waiting outside it. I take my hand from his hurriedly. I know the minute Evelyn sees us together she's going to be asking enough questions. I could do without the extra attention. He looks down at his bereft hand in shock. Only now we're too close to the gang for him to say anything.

'Hi!' I say to everyone, far too cheerily.

'Where the hell have you been?' Evelyn hisses at me, her face murderous. Jesus, someone needs to take a chill pill. I was looking forward to it until now. I hope she doesn't plan on babysitting me the whole night, keeping me away from Jack.

I turn, heading towards the bus in an attempt to avoid Evelyn's pointed stare. She grabs my arm as I try to pass her.

'Not so fast, Miss humps.'

I turn to stare at her with raised eyebrows. 'Miss humps?'

She smirks, hand on her hip. 'As in you were practically humping Jack in the pool earlier. Gosh, everyone could see. Do you have no shame?'

God, I hate how she can make me feel like shit. I look down at my sandal clad feet, as if I've just been told off by the headmistress. Didn't we go over this shit earlier?

'Leave her alone, will you,' Brooke calls, standing next to me in solidarity. Thank God. She must have been listening out. That girl's got my back. 'If she wants to hump people in the pool she can.'

I smile back gratefully, but wish she'd lower her voice. If Jack overhears I'll die. Actually die.

Evelyn raises her eyebrows. 'Erica, you know I wouldn't give a shit about you humping some random.'

That's a total lie; she'd still tell me to stop acting like a slut in public. 'But this is Jack we're talking about. What the hell are you doing getting mixed up with him again?'

'I'm not getting mixed up with him again,' I retort defensively, arms wrapped around myself.

She raises her eyebrows. 'So, thrusting your vag back onto his junk isn't putting out desperate vibes?'

'Hey!' I shout, instantly pissed. How dare she call me desperate. 'We went through this earlier. But we have history. It's natural that we'd be drawn together.'

She shakes her head in dismay. 'The little shit broke your heart. You should be staying the hell away from him, not rubbing yourself against his cock.'

I stop dead in my tracks and turn to her. 'Look, Evelyn, whatever I do on this holiday is my business. I'm stressed enough as it is. The last thing I need is you getting in my face about it, telling me what to do.'

Her face twists in hurt. 'Even if I'm trying to protect you from making the same mistake twice?'

'Yes!' I shout defiantly. 'I'm a big girl, I can make my own decisions and make my own mistakes.'

She scoffs. 'You're supposed to learn from your mistakes! Not repeat history.'

'Who says I'll fucking regret it? Huh?' I shout. 'I'm not an emotional fifteen year old anymore.'

She scoffs with an eye roll. 'Yeah, next thing you'll

be telling me you can get with him this holiday and not let feelings get in the way.'

'Why not?' Brooke asks, intervening. 'I do it all the time.'

She glares back at her. 'Yes, well Erica isn't you Brooke! And this isn't just some dude. This is her first love. There's no way on this earth she'll be able to do anything with that boy and not fall head over heels.'

That boy? He's no longer a boy, he's a bloody man!

'Just drop it Evelyn.' She raises her eyebrows at me again. 'I mean it, Evelyn. Leave me the hell alone over this.'

'If you could start loading onto the bus now please,' an organiser with a clipboard says.

I turn to Evelyn. 'Gladly.'

Jack

The villagers in the mountains are supposed to be making us a traditional meal tonight and putting on some kind of dancing show. I just hope the food isn't gross.

I don't know what the fuck is wrong with me tonight. I had no intention of walking to her room, but I just found myself there. It was like my hand was going to knock of its own accord. And then I couldn't help holding her hand. I'm giving her the wrong messages, I know. Letting her think we can be something in real life, when we can't.

We load the bus, our overweight tour guide shouting, 'Good evening!' to each of us in his thick accent.

The minute I set foot on the bus I spot her sat towards the back, my eyes locking with hers. Shit, she's looking at me with so many questions behind those eyes. Questions I can't answer. I'm such a shit. I sit down two rows in front of her. Crap, why did I have to make it awkward between us?

I take a quick discreet look back and notice Evelyn turn to her with a look that says "see, he's still a silly little boy".

I want to stick my tongue out like a toddler, but I hold myself back.

The coach starts driving along, but my God, this driver must be pissed or something. He's driving like a lunatic! We pass fields, crops, and people walking with donkeys. This is the type of shit I was expecting. Not the well-developed resort we're staying in. We drive around corners of the cliffs, barely missing plummeting to our death.

Every time I look at the others, they've all got the same pale face I imagine I have. Erica looks like she's going to pass out. I want to go to her and wrap her in my arms, but it would raise far too many questions.

We go through a small town filled with dilapidated houses and finally stop outside a whitewashed wall with red tile roof.

The minute we're off the bus, loud folk music assaults my ears. Jesus! And it sounds like it's live. Great. A line starts forming outside a wooden gate.

'I cannot wait for this!' Molly cheers, practically jumping up and down in excitement. Jeez, we've only been here a few days and already her super positive outlook is starting to grate on me.

Alice and Erica roll their eyes. At least I'm not alone.

I stand a few people behind her in the queue. I desperately want her to look around just so I get an excuse to look at her face, but it's as if she's deliberately making sure not to turn her head. Probably pissed off that I held her hand and then decided not to sit next to her on the bus. It's fucking torture, but it's for the best. I can't let her think I'm into her. When, you know, I totally am.

The gates open and a woman wearing a white shirt, black waistcoat, and skirt offers us a tray of what looks like mini poppadum's, encouraging the dip. I take it, too polite to refuse, and throw it into my mouth. Fuck, that's gross. Like mint, lavender and...is that melon? Bitter and vinegary. The tour guide is filming us so I force it down with a smile.

A guy is standing next to the woman. He's dressed in

a white embroidered shirt, playing what looks like a sort of bagpipe. It's blaring out a ridiculously folky song. Cut it out mate.

Next, we're offered a drink called Orujo, poured into a little clay pot, like a shot. I take it, but look at it dubiously. The last time I did shots that I wasn't sure about I ended up being shaken awake by a cleaner on a train.

'Spanish fire water!' the waiter says excitedly. 'Very, very good.'

Erica's suddenly by my side, taking one. I can't chicken out now. I lock eyes with her before downing it. She swallows before knocking hers back.

'You know what we call that drink?' the tour guide asks me, a big stupid grin on her face.

'Err, no,' I admit, smiling at Erica comically.

'It's Spanish viagra!'

She bursts out laughing. Shit. Nothing like being told you've just done Viagra and might have a hard cock all night, to really embarrass you. I can feel my cheeks redden, but I try to shrug, styling it out as best I can.

Evelyn takes her hand, pulling her away. 'Come on, let's get some wine,' she says with warning in her eyes.

Why is she always so up in our business?

We're given small clay jugs to fill up with wine from kegs, or we can pay for beer. Free wine it is then. We find our seats under a covered courtyard. There's a large fire roaring in the centre, rugs hung from the walls, and lanterns flickering. The sun is already starting to set and my stomach tells me I need to eat soon or I'm going to be shit-faced.

The gang sit down with us next to a long rectangular table. Erica is at the opposite end. Every time I look up she's staring at me, but then quickly looks away. It's getting my dick hard. Well, that or the Viagra drink.

The food smells lovely but tastes disgusting. The others eat some of it but I can just about stomach eating some of the sour tasting bread. I end up filling up on wine which I know I'm going to regret later.

A band dressed in all black come on stage. The main singer is wearing a long black leather coat making her look like a Matrix reject. They start playing a Benny Hill song. Well that's a weird bloody choice.

Soon Spanish dancers come out in black trousers and white shirts, holding sticks and wearing the most random masks with long pointed noses. Well, that's slightly terrifying. Bells jingle every time they move. It's a bit like Morris dancing. I wonder if they stole it from us or the other way around?

Some milkmaid looking women with bushy eyebrows join them, skipping along next to them. They start swinging their partners around like they're country and western dancing. Sweet baby Jesus, if this is what Spanish courting is like here, how can anyone be arsed getting laid? Goes on forever.

If I never hear an accordion for the rest of my life it'll be too soon. They drag us up from the table and make us all hold hands, dancing around in a long circle. I look to who's got my hand and see that it's Erica. I grin. I don't know whether it's the Viagra water or the buckets of wine I've had, but I feel myself pulling her away from everyone as we round a corner.

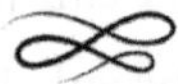

Erica

He pulls me into a dark corner and crushes me against the wall, pinning me with his hips. I barely get a chance to look into his glorious face, attempting desperately to keep my emotions under control, before he's kissing me. It happens quickly, but the kiss itself isn't rushed. It's patient, slow and deep. I open my mouth, encouraging his tongue to move past my lips and tangle with mine. Holy fuck, he's only got better at kissing. I didn't think it was possible.

His hands are tenderly wrapped around my face, causing my cheeks to tingle. It's as if he's cherishing me. It makes my stomach curl up and purr in delight.

After what feels like nowhere near long enough, he pulls his face back, a wide smile on it. I pant, completely out of breath. I wonder if I've actually been holding it?

'Sorry, but I couldn't last any longer.' His voice is husky and he appears out of breath. At least it's not just me.

'Th...that's okay,' I mumble, like an idiot. Way to look intelligent, Erica.

He smiles endearingly at me. 'Come on. Before they notice we've gone.' He grabs my hand and seamlessly integrates us back into the line of hand holders, leaving me no time to process what the hell just happened. Does this mean he's into me? Or just presently horny?

We all break off into normal dancing, a lot more pissed than when we arrived. Jack and the boys sit at the table, being typical moody men. I can't help glancing back every now and again. Every time I do he's watching me. It's like I can feel my face glowing in delight every time I catch him. I put an extra shake into my hips just for him.

'Right,' Alice says, grabbing my hand and looking at me before frantically checking her watch. 'The coach is picking us up soon. I suggest we get as rat-arsed as possible so we don't have panic attacks.'

I know she's only half joking; she's a nervous passenger at the best of times. I'm worried myself. That was him driving in daylight. Now it's pitch black I dread to think how shocking the journey will be.

'Ooh good plan.'

We fill our jugs up as high as we can and use our water bottles so we can bring some with us for the journey. By the time the tour guide finds us to tell us that there is fire walking before loading onto the bus, everyone is three sheets to the wind.

Whoa, I suddenly feel shit-faced myself; like I've been hit by a bus. I stagger out, following the others who stand around the embers of the gone out fire. Jack grabs my hand, pulling me discreetly beside him. He glances up at the sky.

'Look at the stars, Eric.'

I glance up, but I'm not looking at the beautiful starlit sky; I'm watching him taking them all in. He's always had a thing about stars.

'Hey, do you remember when we first stargazed?' he whispers in my ears.

I nod, flushing at the memory of it.

A couple of nights into our caravan holiday we'd hatched a plan to escape the parents and went into Burnham-On-Sea's small high street. We got served in a bar before the manager arrived and busted us. On our way home we cut through the graveyard to get back quicker. It was uphill so I insisted on sitting for a second on a bench.

He'd gazed up at the stars, his arm wrapped around my shoulders.

'Look at the stars, Eric.'

I'd laughed internally. Was that his best chat up line?

'I thought they were aeroplanes,' I said, attempting to be funny.

He burst out laughing. 'Please tell me you're joking?' he asked, his forehead creased in worry.

I burst out laughing too. 'Of course I'm joking.'

I tried to collect myself, watching as a smile curved the corners of his mouth. Moonlight shimmered across his skin, highlighting him in an almost ethereal glow. His eyes locked deeply with mine, a meaningful gleam in them. My heart pounded loud in my ears. Was he going to kiss me?

I wanted so badly to close the little distance between us, to reach out and touch his lips, but the potential rejection stopped me. He reached out and wrapped a loose tendril of my hair around his thumb. My heart spluttered hyperactively. Oh Jesus, that felt like heaven!

He rested his thumb under my chin, cupping my cheek with his palm. I made a strange kind of squeaky noise. My body's way of physically swooning. Please touch me, I begged him psychically.

He pulled my face slowly towards him, his face lowering. I couldn't remember how to breathe. He was going to kiss me and I was going to pass out from deprivation of oxygen.

I closed my eyes, unable to bear being so close to him. Please kiss me. And then his lips were on mine. His warm, plump lips warming up my cold ones. I kissed him back as best I could, but it's hard when you're still in shock. He kissed the corner of my mouth then continued to leave a trail of kisses up to my ear and then back again. Jesus, he was smooth.

And just like that I was in love.

'Watch!' a Spanish man shouts, pulling me back into the present. I watch as he runs over the fire embers. His face is a picture. This doesn't look so much an act, more a form of torture. The things they'll do to try and please the tourists.

'Woo!' I shout along with the crowd, cheering them on.

'She likes it,' the man says pointing at me with a chuckle, his beer belly jumping up and down. Before I can register what's happening he's picking me up and holding me upside down, my head so close to the burning embers that I feel the heat on my face.

'Aaarrgh! Put me down, put me down!' I yelp, closing my eyes in terror.

The crowd is laughing. Yeah, yeah, it's bloody hysterical when someone gets attacked by a random Spanish man. My stomach lurches violently. I've never been good upside down. I once went on a rollercoaster that did it and I ended up spewing so bad I covered several people in it. What a way to ruin my eighth birthday party.

'Get off her!' someone roars from behind me. New arms are around my stomach and my view spins round again. I shake my head to try and refocus myself. I'm looking into Jack's face. He saved me.

'Are you okay?' he asks, concern evident in his eyes as he scans over my body.

'Err..yeah.' Is it weird that I suddenly feel on the edge of bursting into tears? It must be the shock.

'Come on.' He guides me over to the bus, his arm around my waist. I drag in an unsteady breath at the feel of his hand on me.

I can't help but think that this is a very boyfriend thing to do. When in reality I've just dumped my boyfriend at home by email. God, I'm a whore.

We get on the bus and head for the back row. Two seats seem to be missing but we still fit Alice and Charlie with us by the windows seats. Alice gets our bottles filled with wine out and hands mine to me.

'Thanks, but I think I'm already a bit too drunk,' I admit, not meeting Jack's eyes. Definitely far too drunk as I'm imagining licking him from head to toe. And I don't even like toes!

'Suit yourself,' she laughs, already opening hers and taking a few glugs.

The bus starts abruptly, flinging us all back in our seats.

'Jesus!' Charlie chuckles. 'This driver's had more wine than Erica.'

'Hey!' I slur. Shit, he's right.

We swing round a corner, my chair sliding me all the way to the window.

'Shit!'

Everyone bursts out laughing as I swing back as he takes an opposite corner.

'What the hell is with this bus?' I laugh so hard I snort, which just makes everyone laugh all the more hysterically.

The next corner is even more severe, I slide away and then back with such force my head plants itself into Jack's lap. I'm mortified!

'Ooh, cheeky!' Jack chuckles, helping me up. Tom looks back at us and starts wolf-whistling.

'Shit, sorry,' I apologise, cheeks reddening as I remove myself from his groin area. I look away from his face, trying to find words. 'This chair is a nightmare.'

'It's fine,' he says, offering me his hand.

I take it, not sure where he's leading me but find it's to sit on his lap. Well I can't refuse now, can I? I mean, my chair is broken.

'Damn it, Alice, give me that wine,' I demand.

'I told you,' she laughs, handing it over.

I open the lid and start downing it. My stomach is a knotted ball of worry. Every time the bus goes round another corner I'm clinging onto Jack's chest, drinking my wine until it's all gone.

'I swear, I'm going to die on this bus,' I cry, my skin so clammy I'm worried I'm leaving sweat prints on Jack's t-shirt.

He laughs, locking his hazel eyes with mine. 'Do you really think I'd ever let anything happen to you?' His eyes are glinting as if joking, but I know it's just a front. Underneath they're more serious than I've ever seen them.

But the truth remains that I don't really know him anymore. Maybe he'll hurt me again. I don't know anything about this grown up version of Jack. Plus, I'm far too pissed right now to even attempt to dissect it.

'Just rest your head back and try to sleep.' He cups the side of my head and pulls it into his chest. The skin on his hand is silky smooth, no sign of calluses. It makes me wonder what he does for a living. Definitely not a physical job. I wish I hadn't made that stupid rule of skipping all of that info.

I let myself wonder as I sag against him. He wraps his arms around me. A hopeful pain in my chest sprouts, attempting to grow. I squash it back down, determined not to let feelings grow for him. It's hard when his warming citrusy scent soothes my frayed nerves as if he were made to keep me calm.

I let his heartbeat calm me and before long I find myself drifting, him taking all my worries away from me. But still the same thought in my head threatens to ruin it. Can I trust him?

Chapter 8

Erica

Saturday

I wake up in my bed and more importantly I'm alone. I vaguely remember being carried here by Jack, and Brooke cracking some kind of crude joke about him not taking advantage of me while I'm comatose. Shit, I feel hungover. My mouth is as dry as a nun's vagina and my head throbs with the threat of a migraine.

'Come on, sleepy muffin,' Brooke sings, already tying up her bikini. 'It's the water park today.'

'Ugh, I totally forgot about that.'

I'm really not sure how I'm going to cope with throwing myself down water slides when my stomach's this unsettled. The way it's going I could be making my own water slide in the toilet soon enough.

'Come on,' Brooke insists with an eye roll. 'A fry up

will sort you right out.'

'No.' I shake my head. 'I'm not going anywhere and you can't make me.'

Jack

We're sat in the breakfast buffet stuffing our faces with waffles and bacon when Nicholas and Charlie start nodding to each other, as if they're communicating without words. What the fuck is going on?

'Alright, out with it,' I demand, putting down my fork.

Charlie's eyes widen and look to Nicholas.

Nicholas starts chewing on his lip. 'We just think...' he fidgets with his phone.

'They think you should leave twiglet alone,' Tom interrupts. At least he doesn't try and sugar coat crap.

But leave her alone? Why the hell would I leave her alone?

'Why?'

Charlie sighs. 'Look, it's not that we think you should leave her alone. It's just that we don't think you should lead her on if you're not going to offer her anything after this holiday.'

Fuck. When the hell did they get so sensitive to

women's feelings?

'I'm not leading her on. And for all you know she might just want a holiday fling.' I know that's a lie, but I'm clutching at straws here.

Nicholas rolls his eyes. 'Something tells me Erica's not the love them and leave them kind.'

I bloody know that too.

'I mean,' Charlie begins, grimacing, 'we're assuming that you haven't told her about Esme? Or Amber?'

I put my head in my hands. Shit. I know they're right. There's no way we can carry this on in real life. Am I really being a dick and giving her false hope?

'No,' I admit. 'I just...fuck, I can't leave her alone. Having her here at the same time as us. It's just like fate is fucking with me.'

'Hey, we know what you're saying,' Nicholas nods with a frown. 'But if you don't want to tell her the truth, then cut her loose. Don't give her false hope.'

I nod in agreement. It's just a shame that it fucking sucks so hard.

Erica

It seems she can make me. Anything to stop her whining. Most annoying of all, she was right. All of that grease has some sort of magic power. Not that I feel great right now, but it's a start.

By the time we're loading onto the musty bus I'm feeling human again and I'm even a little excited. Especially to be seeing Jack again. Whenever I think of Jack's arms wrapped around me last night I can't help but glow with happiness.

Now that things are over with Karl I feel like I can concentrate on the possibility of me and Jack. I still can't believe we kissed last night. Not that I'm living in a dream world. I have to remind myself that he's probably a player nowadays so I have to make sure to protect myself.

He walks onto the bus with Charlie. I smile up at him, sure he's going to take the empty seat in front of me. My stomach drops when he smiles tightly and instead chooses a seat closer to the driver. What the hell is that all about? Did I do something when I was drunk to piss him off?

Maybe's he's just a bastard and I've been wrong the whole time. Maybe he's moved his sights onto someone else.

As if on cue his phone dings and I watch him as he reads it, his face lighting up with a huge grin. He elbows Charlie and beckons for him to read it. Charlie starts laughing. 'She is so hilarious!' he laughs. Jack can't stop smiling. Who the hell is this whore that's making him laugh so much? What has she got that I haven't?

I cross my arms and turn to look out of the window as we leave the white sandy beach, and ocean, heading slightly more inland. Not that it's built up, but we pass what looks like a farmer's market, which seems quite hip for Luna Island. Then we're on a long carriageway, the blue sky the only prettiness to focus on.

I mean, do I have daddy issues or something? Why have I dumped a perfectly good boyfriend back home for this tool who insists on treating me badly? Maybe my mum's right and I should book in for some therapy when I get back. She keeps telling me I haven't gotten over the diagnosis of her cancer. I myself don't know what there is to get over. All I wanted to know was what treatment she needed to get better.

We make it to the water park in no time. It's far closer to the hotel than I'd thought. Us girls head to the floating ringed area while the boys go straight to the biggest and scariest chutes they can find. I'm glad. I need some time away from Jack.

We've only been floating around for a little while when I notice people staring at me, pointing and laughing. What the hell are they sniggering at?

'Hey, Molly, why is everyone staring at me?'

She lifts her sunglasses up, perplexed, and scans over my body. Her eyebrows hit her hairline in horror.

Oh my God, what is it? Have I got a lizard on me or something? She seems to be wavering, as if torn whether she should tell me.

I follow her eye line down to my breasts, wondering if one's popped out. Even worse, my white bikini has gone completely see-through! Shit! You can see my ruby red nipples!

'Shit!' I quickly cover myself the best I can with my hands.

Alice spots it and bursts out laughing, alerting the others. Yeah, great. That's the last time I buy anything from one of those Facebook boutiques. Cheap as shit material.

Wait a second. If my top is see through...I look down at my crotch. Oh, my ever-loving God! My bikini bottoms are see-through too! You can see my dark pubic hair! Fuck my life!!

I can feel my face turning scarlet. I quickly try to cover myself down there with the palm of my hand, attempting to cling onto some dignity. At least I'm trimmed and neat, rather than my lazy girl bush I normally sport. I cannot believe I am on this ring completely naked. It literally can't get any worse for me.

'Hey twiglet, why you hiding yourself?' Tom shouts over from the side of the pool.

I was wrong; it *can* get worse. And it just has.

I lift one hand to wave him away, but in doing so accidently flash my boobs. Oh fuck! I quickly cover myself back up, every nerve ending in my body screaming in mortification.

'Woah, twiglet! I knew you had a good rack, but fuck if my dick isn't a little hard right now.' He chuckles, loving my discomfort. Sadistic bastard.

I blush crimson, paranoia sweeping over me. How much of them did he see? Shit the bed, I would pay some serious money to be anywhere but here right now.

Jack walks up behind him. 'What are you talking about?'

Tom chuckles, pointing towards me. 'Your girl's got her tits out.'

His girl? How embarrassing! I am *so* not his girl. He didn't even want to smile at me earlier.

His eyes widen in horror, even though I have myself covered. I quickly jump off the hoop, hoping the water camouflages me somewhat. I swim to the edge and press my backside against the wall, covering myself with my hands as best I can.

He walks over, an amused grin on his face. 'Here,' he offers, holding out a towel. 'You can cover yourself with this while you dry off.'

I snort. 'You're assuming I'm willing to get out of the pool at all.'

And what's with the suddenly being nice to me again? He is one confusing bastard. Plus everyone is clearly whispering about me. Some mothers are even shielding their children's faces away from me. I roll my eyes. They'll be the same mothers breastfeeding their four year olds later, no doubt.

'Oh, come on. It's nothing I haven't seen before.' He winks cheekily.

I didn't think it was possible for your cheeks to combust into actual fire, but from the burning sensation I'd say that's exactly what's just happened.

'Well, things have changed since then. And anyway, I don't want the whole water park to see me naked.' Especially not Tom, who's still hovering close by, no doubt waiting for me to exit and flash a tit again.

He titters, clutching onto his stomach. 'Come on. I'll cover you as best I can.' He offers his hand again.

I look at it, considering my very limited options. The girls have hardly run off to get a towel. They seem far too interested in getting a tan. I begrudgingly take it, realising I'm going to have to get out at some time.

'Wait, what about Tom?' I look over and he's still gawking, clearly looking forward to seeing me in all my glory.

Jack turns towards him, puffing out his chest. 'Tom, so help me God, turn the fuck around!' Wow, what's made him so angry? He shouldn't be acting in the tiniest bit protective of me. He's showed today with his bipolar behaviour that I don't mean much to him.

Tom chortles, but turns, as do Charlie and Nicholas. I take Jack's hand and jump out of the pool, quickly covering myself with the towel. Well, this is humiliating.

'Come on.' He guides me with a hand on my waist towards a small tiki bar made from bamboo and straw. Every time he touches me it's as if he sends a trail of tingles up and down my body. It practically hums to be touched more.

'Do you serve any alcohol?' I blurt out before the guy behind the bar even opens his mouth.

'Yes,' he nods with a smile. 'We do sangria.'

'Then two sangria's,' Jack says with a friendly smile.

'Each,' I add quickly. 'I need to get a little drunk,' I explain to Jack. Hair of the dog and all that.

We get our drinks and sit down on a small bench. The minute I've downed the first one I turn to him, suddenly needing to know if he's seeing anyone. All of this guessing is doing my head in.

'So, the guys said you don't have a girlfriend?'

He stares at me aghast, his head whipping up in interest. 'Did they? Were you asking questions about me?' He jibes me lightly in the ribs. 'Ah, I didn't know you cared.'

'No!' I shriek quickly. Too quickly. God, why did I even bring it up? Now he knows I've been obsessing over him. 'It's just, well, I don't even know how or why, but they said it.' I'm a bumbling fool! Get it together Erica.

'No, I don't have a girlfriend,' he confirms with a shy smile. I wish he'd stop it with the shy smile. It's his secret weapon. The minute he pulls it out I'm putty in his hands.

I shake my head, desperate to clear it from the images of us frolicking on the beach together, sand getting in unmentionable places.

'Why was a girl called Amber calling you then?'

Shut the front door, did that really just leave my mouth? Am I really directly asking him about Amber? I could kill myself right now.

He shrugs. 'She's just a friend.'

'Is she...' I really can't stop myself. It must be the drink. It must have topped up last nights and now I'm drunk as fuck. 'Is she the same Amber from when we were younger?'

He raises his eyebrows. 'You remember her?'

Of course I remember her. The Amber who used to constantly answer his phone when I called him, telling me he was off in a field somewhere. She always made out he was off getting up to no good. It was clear to me she fancied the pants off him. I mean, who wouldn't? She was obviously trying to scare me off.

'Don't you remember how jealous of her I was?'

'No,' he frowns. 'I don't remember you ever saying anything about that.'

'Yeah, well that's because I was fifteen and trying to act cool. Inside I was dying of jealousy. She got to see you every day. I knew she fancied you.'

He rolls his eyes. 'Just like I'm sure David fancied you. Every time I spoke to that douche he tried to warn me off you.'

How could he have been jealous of my mate David?

'Really?' That makes me laugh. He's married with his second child on the way now. 'Well, I'm glad I was able to make you half as jealous as I felt.' Way to sound cool Erica. I could openly slap myself.

'Insanely jealous,' he confirms with a nod, a sweet shy smile on his lips. Oh, well at least he's admitted it wasn't just one-sided. Holy hell, the urge to bite his lip is strong. Resist, Erica. Think of the potential restraining order. That never looks good on a CV.

'So...you're not seeing anyone then?' I can't help but confirm. His blasé attitude is killing me. He was always vague as hell.

He chuckles. 'Nope. No-one serious for a good few years now.'

Thank you God. My shoulders sag in relief. Wow, turns out I've been holding out a lot more hope of a reunion that I'd realised. It must be the sangria.

'What about you?'

Oh shit. Well, I set myself up for that one, didn't I?!

'I'm...' Can I lie? Can I? 'I was sort of...seeing someone,' I admit begrudgingly. 'But I've just broken up with him.' He doesn't have to know it was via email a few days ago. 'It wasn't anything serious.'

Nothing serious? We'd been together eight months? What are you playing at Erica?

'Of course you were,' he says with a smile. 'I never expected someone like you to stay single for long. Our paths have never really been aligned, have they?' He looks at me longingly, licking his lips.

I smile sadly back. He's so right. So then why is it always so hard for us to ignore our attraction? I spot his tattoos and decide for a sharp change in subject.

'What's the story behind your tattoo sleeve?' I ask, reaching out to stroke it, but stopping myself at the last second.

He has a pocket watch with the time twenty minutes past four, surrounded by roses. There's an open locket showing pictures of a man and woman, both seemingly old fashioned.

'Who are they?' I ask, pointing at the locket.

He looks down at it, a sad smile on his lips. 'My grandparents. I got it after they passed away. Found some old pictures of them from when they were younger and fell in love with them.'

I can't help but smile. He's so deep. He's getting more attractive by the second. A guy that loved his grandparents.

I point to the date, barely noticeable over one of the roses. 27/07/2013. What does that date mean to him?

'What's with the date?'

He looks down at it. 'That's the date my life changed forever.' He doesn't look sad, but he frowns, as if immediately clouded with thoughts still plaguing him.

Wait, didn't the guys say something about him not having dated in years. Since. Since something happened. That date is about four years ago. Is that the incident they're referring to? What the hell happened on that date?

'Sorry, I didn't mean to upset you.'

'Oh, you haven't,' he says with a shake of his head, pushing his hair off his face.

I daren't ask him about the lion and elephant in case that means something too.

'Anyway,' he says, clapping his hands together. 'I have the exact thing to cheer you up.'

'Really?' I ask excitedly. Don't act too keen, Erica. Try to play it cool. 'What?'

Shower me with a hundred kisses? Is that too much

to ask?

'Yep,' he nods. 'Come on. We're going on that water slide.' He points behind us to what looks like the tallest water flume in the park. Scratch that, in the world!

'I don't think so,' I snort, clinging onto my towel.

'Come on, Eric. Where's your sense of adventure?' His eyes sparkle with mischief.

'Sense of adventure? I've already flashed half the water park my tits and vag. I'd say I'm pretty set on adventures for one day! Besides, I'm not letting anyone else see me naked.'

'We'll just wrap this towel around you. Come on, it'll be fun.' He eyes me daringly.

I can't help but smile back at him. 'How is it you can always talk me into doing stupid things?'

He grins. 'Because I'm adorable.'

I roll my eyes.

He stands up. 'Come on, flasher. Let's do this.'

Jack

I meant to stay away from her, I really did. But fuck, that girl's just too hard to ignore. Especially when she's flashing her bits for everyone to see. It didn't look like anyone else was running to her rescue, so I had no choice but to help her out with the towel and get her a drink to steady her nerves.

Yes, I know I shouldn't have suggested the water slide, but it's as if she's addictive. Every time I get a little hit, I'm not satisfied, I just want more. And the look on her face when I suggested it was too adorable. She's scared shitless, but she's still let me talk her into it. I love having that power over her.

And I mean, it's not like I'm making out with her. I've saved her from an embarrassing situation and now I'm attempting to cheer her up. It's not like I've proposed marriage. Besides, the more I think about it, the more I think the guys are overreacting. And even if we did only get this holiday, I can't help but want to grab at it with both hands. Look how long I've replayed that holiday fifteen years ago in my head. If this will give me another fifteen years of good memories, then I want to take it.

I'm a selfish bastard and I know it. But if being selfish means keeping that smile on Erica's face, then I'm a big selfish fucker.

Erica

It's too high. It's too bloody high. Every time I look down I feel like I'm going to fall off the side of the earth. I have the urge to get down on my hands and knees and cling onto something.

'Come on Eric,' Jack says eagerly. 'The guy says its fine for you to go down with the towel wrapped around you as long as you hold it tight.'

I snort. 'Like I'd willingly let it go.'

'Come on then. What are you waiting for?' He's so excited bless him.

'I...' I look down again, scrunching my eyes shut as a fresh wave of nausea washes over me.

'Don't be scared Eric. I did it earlier. It's amazing. The rush is immense!'

I try to gulp down the panic. If I don't do this now I never will. It's not like I can just turn around and walk back down the millions of steps past the other waiting people. That would get me killed for sure. At least this will give me something else to focus on when I think back to this disastrous day.

'Okay, let's do this,' I say, my tongue shaking so much my words are barely audible.

'That's my girl.'

Oh, God, is it wrong that that very sentence makes my heart skip a beat?

I position myself at the top of the chute, holding the towel tightly around myself.

'Ready?' the guy running the chutes yells to us,

holding his thumb up in excitement.

Jack grins back at me. I'd do anything to get that grin. Apparently even throw myself off the highest water slide in the world.

'Three, two, one, go!'

I let myself slip down in a brief moment of braveness. It's not long lived. I'm immediately thrust down, the slide going completely vertical. I lose grip of the towel almost straight away, it flies over my head. I splutter, the heavily chlorinated water spraying into my face. Sunshine blasts through now and again as sections open to the blinding sunlight.

I'm tossed and turned round corners so violently my stomach contracts in fear. This is it. I'm going to die of a heart attack in this very chute. They'll find me dead at the bottom. My lifeless body floating about, my tits and vag on display for all to see.

Then I'm flung from it, falling, nothing beneath me. I scrunch my eyes shut before my body plunges into water, it shooting straight up my nostrils.

I flail my arms around, desperate to get to the top where sunlight beckons. My head finally emerges allowing me to spit and splutter out the water I've swallowed. I swim to the edge, conscious of Jack waiting there for me. I start to lift myself out but Jack's eyes nearly bulge out of their sockets.

'Erica!' he shrieks, swimming over to me. 'Do NOT try and get out of this pool again.'

'Why not?' I ask, desperate to get out and go back to the hotel. I've had too much trauma for today. For a bloody lifetime.

'Because your bikini top isn't on your body anymore.'

I look down and shit, he's right. I quickly cover myself up as he swims over, I'm assuming, to find it. There's no point. Has he forgotten it's bloody see-through anyway? Cheap piece of shit.

'Where's my towel?' I shriek. 'It's the towel I need.'

Why is my life such a fuck up?

He comes back over with my soaking wet towel which he wraps round me, his palm grazing my boob.

'Shit, sorry,' he apologises, his cheeks flushing.

I nod awkwardly. He lifts himself out of the pool and helps me.

'Jesus, Eric. You're never far from drama, are you?'

Chapter 9

Jack

Whenever I think of today I can't help but laugh. Erica is so fucking unlucky. It's beyond adorable. Seeing her tits on display like that was too fucking much. I had to immediately jump into the main pool so she wouldn't see my raging boner.

And the thought of someone else seeing her tits made me murderous. I don't want anyone else seeing what's mine. Shit, what am I saying? She's not mine. And that fact alone makes me desperate to have her.

I have to have her close. What the fuck is it about this girl? Every time I'm around her I can't reason with my cock to calm the fuck down. I keep telling myself it's just memories but I know it's more than that. When I'm not with her I'm counting down the time until I see her again.

Right now I want to see her more than anything. So,

that's how I find myself outside of her hotel room, desperately trying to think up an excuse to talk to her. The only thing I can think of is asking her if she's coming to the club tonight.

I've put my hand up to knock three times and each time I've chickened out before my knuckles have hit the wood. This time I'm going to do it. I take a deep breath and knock. Brooke stands there in her bikini with a bag in her hand.

'Oh...hey.'

I hadn't prepared myself for someone else answering the door.

Her confused face quickly lights up with mischief. Uh-oh. I really don't know how to take Brooke. She seems like a man-eater.

'Err...is Erica here?'

Before she's had a chance to respond I hear Erica from inside.

'B, don't forget to do me before you go.'

WHAT did she just say? My dick twitches.

She comes into vision, looking up and realising I'm here. 'Oh...' she blushes. Fuck, she's adorable. In just her bikini like earlier, except now not a see through one, holding some sort of pot.

Brooke grins a wide shit-eating grin. 'I'm just on my way out to get ready with Molly, but I'm sure Jack here can help you.'

She practically skips past me. I put my hands in my shorts pockets and rock on my heels, the awkwardness too much to bear. When I look up at Erica, she thankfully seems just as embarrassed.

'Do you...' I clear my throat. 'Do you need help?'

Erica

I wake up from my nap, thinking that I haven't had much sleep at all. When I look at my phone I see that I did actually get an hour in. Better than nothing. Brooke's blow-drying her hair in the corner. That must have woken me up.

Fuck, I'm hot. Not just from the weather. Whenever I think of Jack I have to squeeze my thighs together to stop me from dripping on the tiles, or worse giving in and finger fucking myself under the covers so Brooke doesn't see. But knowing her she'd probably catch on, whip the sheets off to prove it and laugh her arse off. Yeah, a *bit* off putting.

'Hi, sleepyhead.'

'Hi. I need to exfoliate before I get in the shower.' I yawn, exhausted at the idea.

'Okay. Well I'm just about to leave to do Molly's

hair.' There's a knock at our door. 'That's probably her, getting all impatient.'

Probably. Excitable little bunny she is.

'Okay.' I run towards the bathroom. 'But don't go before helping me.'

If I don't exfoliate every day on holiday I start peeling and lose all of my tan. I grab my pot of scrub and strip down to my bikini, scooping my hair up into a messy top knot so it doesn't get all gunky.

I can hear her talking so I walk out of the bathroom, still doing up the bikini string on the side of my briefs.

'Don't forget to do me before you go.' I look up to see Jack at the door, an amused grin on his face. 'Oh...'

Brooke looks between us both, grinning widely. 'I'm just on my way out to get ready with Molly, but I'm sure Jack here can help you.'

Jack puts his hands in his pockets and rocks on his heels. Could this get any more embarrassing?

'Do you...' he clears his throat. 'Do you need help?'

I cough, my mouth suddenly dry. 'What are you doing here?'

He smiles, dragging his hand through his hair. 'I was just wondering if you guys were coming to the club tonight? But now I want to see Brooke *do you*.' He grins devilishly.

A thick tension fills the air, it crackling in my ears.

Brooke gives me a brief wave, wink and then she's out the door, leaving me to deal with this myself.

'So...you need help?'

Yeah, I need help. To calm my self the fuck down so I don't swallow my own tongue. I mean, shit. Here I am thinking I'm safe in my own hotel room and then all of a sudden Jack walks in offering to help exfoliate me.

I know it's wrong, but I want to say yes. My vag is practically begging me to. The thought of his hands on me irresistible.

'Err...I was just going to exfoliate, but don't worry about it.'

'No, I'll help,' he grins, licking his lips. Those gorgeous lips. I want to feel them on me again.

'Um...okay.' How am I going to cope with him touching my body? I'll probably explode from lust. 'We should...probably do it in the bathroom.'

He grins deliciously. Oh Jesus, if I looked up panty wetting smile in the dictionary there'd be a picture of Jack right now.

'The exfoliating,' I add quickly, sure where his dirty mind is going.

He nods, placing his hand out. 'After you.'

I take a discreet deep breath and walk into the bathroom. I bet he's checking out my arse. This is awful. How the hell did I get myself into this situation?

I point to the pot of exfoliator as I put it down next to the sink. 'If you could do my back? You know, the hard to reach areas.'

'No probs.' He's trying to sound casual, but his breathing has changed and his voice sounds huskier.

Our eyes meet, nervous energy bouncing between us. I rip my eyes from him and turn so my back is facing him. I scoop my hand into the pot and start massaging the goop onto my arms. I see him in my peripheral vision scooping some out of the pot.

My heart pounds, anticipating his touch. Dear God, just knowing his hands are going to be on my skin any minute has me creaming my knickers. Get a hold of yourself, Erica!

Then his hands are on the top of my shoulders. Fuck, my breathing's laboured just from this. He must be able to hear in this deafening silence. I swallow, my mouth suddenly dry.

His hands remain completely still for a few seconds, the heat from them relaxing my tense muscles. I stop myself from openly moaning like a wanton whore. I take a discreet deep breath, attempting to relax. His hands move, massaging the exfoliator gently into my skin.

Gosh almighty, it's heavenly. I have to bite my tongue to stop myself crying out his name. How can I be this horny? I haven't had the horn this bad for years.

I force myself to carry on exfoliating myself. I take some more goop and bend over to do my legs. My ass bumps straight up against his erection - holy moly! He's turned on too? Well, this is awkward. I have to quickly remind myself that I'm working it into my legs and shouldn't pull my bikini to one side so he can fuck me. Erica, have some class!

Slowly, ever so painfully slowly, his hands travel down my back, every nerve ending singing in praise, until they're in the shallow of it. I ignore my own sterner self and find myself "accidentally" bumping my arse against him. Against it. I don't know if I'm trying to encourage him or what the hell I'm thinking but it seems to do the job. His hands move down my back and now they're circling my hips. Ideas of him gripping onto them while he pounds into me from behind invade my mind. Damn it, focus Erica.

As if reading my mind, he grasps them. I might not be able to see his face but I can sense his desperation. I feel powerful knowing I can have this effect on him. When we were teenagers I always felt like the ugly duckling. Now I know I'm hot. *Note to self: must widen doors at home to fit head through.*

They swoop up again. Jesus, this feels beyond erotic.

'Is this okay?' he asks, his husky voice having the same effect on me as a bottle of wine.

'Mmmhhmmm.' I nod frantically, unable to form anything more coherent.

I have to carry on. Get this over and done with as quickly as possible. No use torturing myself. I grab some more out of the pot, careful not to move so much that his hands come off me. I'm a bloody glutton for punishment.

I force myself to carry on with one leg, my trembling hands slowly working their way up. I make sure to press his erection into my butt as much as possible. It's so close to being near where I want it most. So close, yet so far.

I straighten myself up and massage my stomach. I'm really just prolonging it now, desperately needing for his hands to remain on me. I'm already sad about when they'll leave.

His hands massage back up my spine in figures of eight and up to my shoulders. His fingers sprawl over my shoulders wrapping their way around my throat, then caressing down until he's massaging the very top of my boobs.

I find myself pushing out my tits, desperate for him to touch them. They've never ached like this before. I always assumed I wasn't an "achy breasts" kind of gal. But here I am, aching. I clearly just needed Jack.

Please touch them I will silently. My nipples are hard as rock, throbbing so much I'm surprised they're not making an audible sound.

His hands meet in the middle of my upper chest. I hold my breath. Please touch me. His fingers skirt down the centre of my boobs, careful not to touch them, and onto my stomach. Goddammit. Does he know that he's teasing me? I'm tempted to raise a white flag and beg.

His hands sweep up under my arms only for them to circle around my boobs again, avoiding contact where I want it the most. This is fucking agony. I groan in frustration. Shit, I hope he didn't hear.

I get some more from the pot and start on the other leg, bending as far over in invitation as I can. He pulls me back by my hips until I'm as pressed onto him as possible. Fucking hell. This is getting ridiculous. My bikini bottoms are soaking.

I stand up straight, my back flush against his front, his body warmth melting my last shred of resistance. My breath comes out in short, sharp bursts as his hands travel down the sides of my breasts and then wrap around my stomach, pulling me back even further into him. So close I can feel his breath on my neck.

His hands travel back up my sides until they're at the string of my bikini top. He stills his fingers there for a moment, as if asking permission. I stay silent. I have a fear that if I talk, say anything at all, I'll ruin this moment for both of us. And I'll do anything to make sure it doesn't stop.

'Is this okay?' he asks as he slowly unties the string, loosening the bikini so it only hangs around my neck.

'Y...y...yes,' I mumble, like an incoherent fool.

Painfully slowly his hands travel around the front and cup my breasts. I moan like a wanton little whore. I can't help it. Apparently that's all the encouragement he needs. He kneads one while pinching the other, rolling it between his thumb and forefinger. I drop my head back in pleasure, it landing on his chest. He takes the opportunity to bite my neck greedily.

'Gooooooooood!' I'm going to come on the spot if he carries on like this.

But wait, is it weird that we're doing all of this without even kissing? He pinches my nipple and I buck against him. Oh, who fucking cares.

He lifts my bikini top off over my head. This feels too good to ignore.

You'll regret it.

Damn that sensible voice in my head. Probably Evelyn having somehow wormed her way in there. I push it to the back of my brain, instead arching my back and pushing my boobs into his hands more.

I reach out behind me and wrap my arm around his neck. He plants a quick kiss on my palm. He's so adorable. I grind my butt against him, reminding myself that he's massive. Another reason not to have sex with him. He'd probably ruin me. Stretch me out like an old handbag and ruin me for other men. Doesn't stop my V wanting the D though.

One of his hands snakes down and pulls at the bikini string of my bottoms. Thankfully I was never a girl scout, so it unravels easily. He trails a finger over my folds as he kisses me passionately on the neck. I need more. I can't take it.

It does worry me slightly that he's still got exfoliant on his fingers. I mean, I'm sure that stuff isn't supposed to go into your hoo-hah. But maybe, it'll just mean I'll have an exfoliated noonoo. It can't be a bad thing, right? Who cares?

'Please,' I beg him, not sure what I'm even asking for at this point.

He chuckles darkly, moving so he's massaging my clit. I lose all train of thought. All I can do is feel and want. Most guys I've been with go at it like it's a light switch, smashing it relentlessly, but this guys a pro. He's gentle and teasing instead. The micro-bubbles from the exfoliator only heighten the sweet heavenly sensation.

He slips his greedy fingers into me, two at once. I gasp, expecting to have to give myself a moment to warm up, like I normally do. But I'm so embarrassingly wet they glide in easily, too easily. I hope he doesn't think I'm a bucket. It's just that I'm so turned on.

'We should get you washed up,' he whispers in my ear, his voice deep and gruffly.

Oh no, is he trying to end this? All I can do is nod. He throws his top off. I help him finish undressing by dragging his swimming shorts down. Jesus, the sight of him! It's the most beautiful dick I've ever seen. I wrap my hands around it and squeeze. It's velvety soft.

He grabs me around the waist and lifts me up, so quickly I almost fall from dizziness. I instinctively wrap my legs securely around him. He walks me into the shower, hitting random buttons to get it working.

A burst of freezing cold water hits us. I scream, my nipples going rigid in response. He smiles apologetically

'Sorry.' He's ridiculously sweet considering the nature of what we're doing. He turns the dial on the shower so that warmer water starts pumping out.

He sucks one breast into his mouth, his tongue circling round my erect nipple, soothing it back to life with his warm delicious tongue. I wrap my arms tighter around his neck, scared of slipping and take my chance to kiss his neck. It feels divine. I ache so bad down below. I really want him inside me. No, I *need* him inside me.

He grabs my hips, leaning back slightly to rip off my bikini bottoms. He turns so my back is pressed up against the wall, lines his dick up against me, searching into my eyes for some kind of permission. I'm so hot and bothered under the now almost boiling water. All I can do is nod.

He thrusts into me, balls deep within a second. Shit!

'Agh!' I scream involuntarily.

He's so fucking deep, it feels like he might be in my womb. I look up to him in shock, my eyes no doubt holding a small percentage of the vulnerability I feel right now. He presses his forehead against mine, panting heavily. It gives me a minute to collect myself. I take a deep breath, attempting to customise to his size.

'I'm okay,' I nod, wanting him to move.

He leans back before thrusting into me again, over and over, relentlessly as he nips at my neck. Each thrust causes me to scream. The feeling is beyond heavenly. The roughness of the sex mixed with the gentle pouring water has me trembling. It's a fabulous mix of pleasure and pain.

His thrusts get more demanding, deeper still, until I feel dirty and raw. His eyes don't leave mine. So many words left unspoken between us.

A hot sensation throbs down below, slowly travelling up my body until the hairs on the back of my neck are standing on end. My thighs ache from the position but that only seems to heighten my pleasure.

A tingling starts, spreading all the way up to my neck. Every muscle in my body feels like it's contracting as my stomach tightens into a hard ball. Hell, I need to come. I need to release before I physically explode.

As if realising I'm close he changes position so his back is against the shower wall rather than mine. My back falls further back, deepening him inside me. *Fuck!* I'm going to come so fucking hard. I'm wound so tight I'm clutching onto his hair for dear life, pulling at the roots.

The pressure keeps building, riding me so high it's as if I'm having an out of body experience. Waves start washing over me, until it hits me, as if out of the blue.

My body wracks with tremors, waves running up and down my body, releasing my muscles. I clench my eyes shut as my body begins to spasm uncontrollably, swear words spilling from my mouth.

'Open your eyes,' he demands in a whisper.

I open them, embarrassed by my own groans which are so far away from my control right now. The feeling finally dissipates, replaced by a soothing, calming balm. My legs suddenly feel like lead, dropping down from around his waist.

I collapse, every muscle in my body giving up. He carries me down gently to the floor of the shower, stopping me from hurting myself.

He lifts my knees so they're by my shoulders as he takes a few final thrusts, before he grunts in my ear, coming inside me. Shit, we really should have worn a condom.

I've only recently come off the pill because it was giving me migraines. Not that I can mention that now. His body weight collapses on top of me, his laboured breathing unsteady against my ear.

The pleasure quickly escapes out of my body, instead replaced with fear. Fear that now I'll have to face up to what we've just done. Will it be awkward? Should I get the morning after pill?

He leans back, avoiding my gaze. Oh God, it's started. The awkward brush off. He takes my hand and helps me up to standing. Maybe not. Maybe I'm just panicking.

I watch as he cleans himself off under the shower spray. I self-consciously copy him, washing off any remains of our dirty encounter.

He steps out of the shower and grabs a towel which he wraps around his waist. He grabs another one and wraps it around me, all the time avoiding my gaze. I'm so confused. He's looking after me like a gentleman, but why is he not looking at me? Does he regret it?

We walk back into the bedroom, an eerie silence surrounding us. I sit down on the edge of the bed.

'So...' I look up to catch what's going to come out of his mouth next. He's either going to say it was a huge mistake or that he had a great time. 'You're coming tonight, right?'

I smile at the possible euphemism.

'Attending,' he quickly corrects, grabbing his shorts and pulling them on. 'You're attending tonight. Aren't you?'

'Yeah,' I nod. 'I'll be there.'

'Good. I'll see you then, then.' Is he feeling awkward too? He sure as hell sounds it.

I nod and watch as he turns and hurriedly leaves. This is just casual for him. Just a fuck. It doesn't mean the same thing to him as it does to me. I'm such a stupid cow. And now I'm going to have to take the morning after pill.

And then he's gone, as if what we did meant nothing.

Oh God. What the hell have we done?

Chapter 10

Erica

I manage to keep myself busy with re-showering, washing my hair and then drying it messily. It never suits me when I try and tame it, it's always better to let it do its own thing and that's normally wild waves.

Each time I've reached for the phone to call Brooke I've talked myself out of it. I can pretend it didn't happen if I don't talk about it. Pretend it was some kind of wild daydream I had.

Of *course* I didn't just sleep with my old holiday flame without discussing why we broke up in the first place. Of *course* I didn't have sex with him without him even kissing me on the mouth. I'm not that whore, right? Oh crap, I totally am and whenever I remember it I have to clench my thighs together to stop myself from getting overly aroused.

How could it have been so great? Like our bodies

were made for each other? Not that it will happen again. I know that it can never go anywhere with him living in a completely different postcode and I'm not the type of girl to agree to being a fuck buddy. I have more class and self respect than that.

I walk down the corridor and knock on Molly's door. Brooke answers.

Her eyes widen, scanning over me. 'Shit, girl, you look hot!'

I roll my eyes with a smile. 'No need to sound so shocked.'

She herself is wearing a neon pink PVC boob tube dress.

'So,' she grins, leaning against the door frame. 'Did you get laid?'

'What?' I say on a gasp, cheeks burning. For once I wish she wasn't so upfront about this stuff. I'm still not ready to talk about it.

'Oh my God, you *so* did!' She jumps up and down, clapping her hands, her boobs nearly breaking free.

'She did what?' Molly asks, appearing in a peach maxi dress, her eyeshadow all smoky and dark. That's why she wanted Brooke's help.

'Our girl got laid,' Brooke says proudly, like a mother at brownies.

'No way!' Molly screams, jumping around herself.

'With Jack I assume?'

'Sssh! Keep your voice down,' I hiss. 'Evelyn can't find out.'

Thankfully she insisted on her own room, rather than sleeping on one of our sofa beds. Bloody diva that she is.

'Why is she so against it?' Molly asks with a heavy sigh. 'I'd never stand in the way of love's young dream.'

I giggle at her use of words. 'Molly, you're the cutest.'

We make our way down to the bar, Brooke having apparently agreed with the guys that we'd meet them there. It makes me feel slightly better. At least I can down a cocktail before I see him, if I'm lucky. I mean, I have no idea what I'm going to say. How he's going to react?

Unfortunately, as we walk in I can see the guys are already here. Shit. I swallow down the panic and try to act calm in front of the girls. Jack glances up and spots me. I freeze in fear. His smile wavers before he looks away. Shit. He just totally dissed me! Am I a shit fuck? Have I got a baggy pussy or something?

'Drinks?' Molly asks us with an eager smile. She's so jolly. I could really do without it right now. I feel like I just want to lock myself in the hotel room and listen to Kelis' *Caught Out There,* singing *I hate you so much right now*, while having a good sob into my pillow.

I begrudgingly follow the girls over towards the guys.

We stand around their high table saying hi. I keep my head down and try to blend in.

'Now listen girls,' Tom says, getting all of our attention. 'I don't want to be a dick, but we don't want you cockblocking us tonight.'

I scoff loudly. Brooke laughs and flicks her hair behind her shoulder. 'Please, more like you guy's cockblocking *us*.'

How can she be so laid back when she's slept with him? I envy how easygoing she is about sex. I wish I could be more like that, rather than chancing a discreet look at him every few minutes.

'Anyway, it would be vagblocking for Molly,' Alice snorts.

The guys all turn simultaneously to stare at Alice, their foreheads wrinkled.

'Huh?' Charlie says, looking around at the others.

Molly's cheeks go red, but she quickly straightens her shoulders. 'What Alice was trying to explain, *terribly*, is that I'm gay.'

The guys look to each other, like she just told them she's into necrophilia.

'As in...you're extremely happy?' Tom asks, seeming serious.

Brooke rolls her eyes. 'As in she licks pussy, dumb arse.'

Charlie's eyes nearly bulge out of their sockets. Bless him. He must have really fancied her.

'Shit, Molls!' Tom shouts with a chuckle. 'Sorry, but I just never had you down as a lesbian.'

'I get that a lot,' she nods, blushing adorably.

'Anyway,' Evelyn claps, 'I think we should split up tonight.' She looks around. 'Stand in different areas. That way we all get a chance.'

'Ooh, on the pull tonight Evelyn?' Alice asks with a bemused face.

'No!' she snaps, before a grin takes over her face. 'Only, well, the barman did say he might come tonight.'

'Oooh!' we all chime childishly before bursting into chuckles. I'm glad someone broke my tension, if only for a second.

I'm glad we're separating. Every time I chance a look at Jack he's laughing along as if nothing's the matter. As if we didn't just have sex earlier. It's actually making me doubt myself. I mean, I didn't dream it, did I? No, he's clearly just a heartless bastard. Some things never change.

We wander off to another table and before long the sexy barman turns up with a bunch of good looking Spaniards. They could be a way to forget Jack. Or make him jealous. Oh for fuck's sake, now I'm resorting to playground tactics. What has happened to me? I'm fifteen again!

'Hi,' one of them says to me, his chestnut eyes warm and friendly.

I smile back politely. 'Hi.' I suppose I can't be rude, can I?

'Where are you girls from?'

'Brighton,' I answer good naturedly, having to shout it in his ear so he can hear me.

I catch something in my peripheral vision and turn to see Jack staring at me, a murderous expression on his face. Oh yeah, he doesn't want me, but he doesn't want anyone else to. What a bloody caveman!

'Brighton girls!' they all cheer. I'm sure they don't have the foggiest where Brighton is, but whatever.

I pretend to cheer back, giggling. I know I'm being stupid, but now the overwhelming urge to see Jack's angry vein in his neck spurs me on. It might be the cocktail in me, but whatever. I deserve some positive attention, dammit.

'Do you want to dance?' the Spaniard asks me.

I look at the others, already on their way to the dance floor with the other guys. Why the hell not.

'Okay,' I nod, taking his outstretched hand. Eww, it's sweaty.

We go to the dance floor where they're playing Demi Lovato's *Cool for the Summer*. He spins me around as if we were on *Strictly Come Dancing*. Who knew the sweaty handed Spaniard had moves?! For a while I'm so busy making sure I don't fall over I forget all about Jack.

This guy seems fun and a perfect gentleman. Maybe I should just forget about Jack and move on. I don't want to waste this holiday stressing over some man. Some manchild in Jack's case. Bloody juvenile idiot. Devastatingly handsome idiot.

A slower R'n'B song comes on and the Spaniard pulls me close. I recognise it immediately; *End of the Road* by Boyz II Men. I love this song! But this is a bit more awkward. I really don't want his hot, sweaty body pressed up against me like this. Especially to one of my favourite songs. I politely push him away, my face uneasy.

'Sorry, I need the loo,' I assert, gesturing towards the toilets.

I turn and flee towards it. I walk into a small foyer area outside the ladies loos; the minute the door bangs shut the atmosphere is calmer. I walk into the bathroom and run my wrists under some cool water. Get a hold of yourself Erica. You can do this.

Forget dancing with this randomer and tell Jack what he's missing out on. I'm a good woman and there's no way I can be that much of a shit shag. He deserves to give me a bit of bloody respect.

That's it; I'm having it out with him. I steel my gaze

in the mirror, attempting to look as scary as possible, but I still notice the vulnerability in my eyes. Dammit, if it was anyone but Jack this would be so different. Things change when you used to be in love with someone.

I hold back my shoulders and walk out. You can be a bad arse bitch, Erica. As long as you believe it.

'Hey.'

I turn, hoping it's Jack waiting outside for me, to find the Spaniard. Oh. Great...not.

'Hi.' I raise an eyebrow in question. Was he waiting for me out here?

He stalks towards me, his eyes predatory. 'I thought we could finish what we started.'

'Huh?'

Before I even have a moment to process it, he's pressed me up against the wall and is crushing his lips against mine. Whoa, where does this guy get off? I fucking danced with him, I didn't propose.

I try to push him off. 'Sorry, but I'm not- '

'Don't worry,' he says, taking my hand and holding it up against the wall above my head. He crashes his lips against mine again, this time so rough that our teeth clash.

I struggle with all my might, but he's a strong fucker. My heart starts racing, thumping loudly in my ears.

How did I get myself into this kind of trouble?

Jack

I can't fucking believe Erica. How can she regret earlier? I thought we were going to have a repeat performance tonight, but when she saw me she froze up, looking terrified. Full of regret. Well, she wasn't complaining when she was screaming my name earlier. That's all I'm saying.

Then she's spent the rest of the night ignoring me and dancing with these local bastards who are sweating so much they look like they've covered themselves in baby oil. She can't honestly find that attractive, right? She must be deliberately trying to piss me off. I just want to grab her and shake out the stupid. I have a feeling I'd be there a while.

I see her go off towards the toilets. Now is my chance to confront her. I need to know what the fuck is going on. Why she's being so cold towards me when I've done nothing wrong. I wait a minute and then casually make my way in.

As soon as I'm outside the toilets I freeze in horror. One of the gross locals has Erica crushed against the wall, leaving no escape, pawing at her. It's obvious by her feeble attempts to push him off that it's not reciprocated.

How fucking dare he.

I've always laughed when people say they saw red. Thought it was a tad dramatic. But I see R.E.D. My blood boils, my hands curling into fists before I grab him by the shoulders and throw him off her.

He turns, surprised, to look up at me. I take the opportunity to punch him in the mouth, then the stomach. I turn to look at her, needing reassurance she's okay. She looks back, eyes wide in vulnerability, tears falling down her cheeks. The fact that he's caused her hurt makes my muscles quiver in fresh rage. I'll kill the fucker.

He storms towards me, clearly having sensed my weakness. He wraps his arms around my stomach and pulls me down to the floor, attempting to punch me in the face. I swerve out of the way just in time.

Erica's suddenly behind him, her face determined. She grabs his ear and twists it. I can't actually believe what I'm seeing! Where the hell did she learn that move?

'Aagh!' the guy shrieks. It gives me a chance to push him off and land another punch on his jaw.

'Get the hell out of here!' I yell. I've never heard myself so mad.

He finally admits defeat, stalking off, slamming the door behind him.

Erica bends down to help me up. I take her hand and

let her help me up to standing. Looking down at her tearstained face makes me want to punch a wall. It's taking all of my remaining strength not to wrap her protectively in my arms, but after earlier I don't know where I stand.

'That was a bit of an overreaction,' she snorts, looking at the floor.

I feel myself turn murderous, baring my teeth like a wild animal. Overreaction? Is she for fucking real? She backs away a step, as if scared.

'Overreaction?' I repeat in horror, my heart beating so quickly I wouldn't be surprised if it jumped out of my chest and punched her straight in the face. 'He had his fucking hands on you! Don't tell me you wanted that?'

She can't possibly have. She's lucky I didn't kill the fucker. How dare he touch what's mine.

'Of course not,' she gasps, her eyes clouding over with hurt, more unshed tears welling up inside them.

'Exactly. That prick was trying to force himself on you. I don't want his filthy fucking hands on you.'

I don't want him anywhere near her. Being in the same country is sounding too much right now. Every muscle in my body is so tense I feel like I need to run right now. Run off the adrenaline coursing through my veins.

Someone walks into the lobby, eyes us and carries on to the toilet. Wise move. Right now someone would only have to look at me wrong for me to put their head down a toilet.

Fuck it. This needs sorting.

I take her arm and guide her gently to the side, so we are stood behind some stacked chairs.

'Why do you care anyway?' she asks, shaking her arm loose from me and crossing both her arms over her chest.

I can't believe her. I thought girls got all mushy and attached after sex, not all defensive and bitchy.

'Are you fucking serious?' I ask in undisguised shock, my neck stiff and achy. 'I had my dick in you only a few hours ago.'

'Romantic way to put it,' she snorts sarcastically.

Whatever. Right now is not the time for me to be picking appropriate words. I'm too fucking worked up.

'And then you're trying to get with that prick right in front of me. What the fuck's that about?'

She sighs, as if suddenly exhausted. She looks up at me, her eyes wide and unsure.

'I'm not a mind reader you know,' she retorts, not meeting my eyes. 'It was weird earlier. You know...after. And then I come here and you look away from me. What the hell am I supposed to think?'

She thinks I looked away? She's the one that froze like I was a massive fucking regret.

'I looked away because you looked horrified at the

sight of me. Doesn't really give a guy confidence, you know.'

'Wait.' She shakes her head, trying to get this straight. 'Are you saying you were going to talk to me tonight, but you thought I didn't want you to?'

Duh.

'Yeah.' Her face brightens up, so brightly I just want to smush her face. 'I liked what happened earlier. I was pretty sure from the way you were screaming that you were enjoying it too.' I smile at the memory.

She turns scarlet and looks down. 'I did. But, I hate all of this awkwardness. I assumed you just wanted to leave it at that.'

I laugh. How is she so naive about this? Can't she see how fucking hot she is?

Ashanti's "Foolish" seeps through the cracks in the door. That song always reminds me of our summer together.

'Eric, now that I've had a taste there's no way I'm going back to just friends.'

I want to have her in my bed every night and fuck her until she can't walk. But I think if I tell her that she'll potentially freak out.

'I think we should keep it quiet,' she says quickly, fidgeting with the edge of her top.

Keep it a secret? Why the fuck would she want to

keep it a secret? I'm a bloody catch.

'Really?' I can't help but hide the hurt from my voice, so I quickly cover it up with a face full of bravado.

'Yeah. I know everyone will ask loads of questions and I can't deal with that. Especially Evelyn. She's told me to stay the hell away from you.'

Fucking Evelyn.

'She's never liked me, has she?' I say, then sigh.. Erica always let her involve herself in our relationship.

'She's just looking out for me,' she says defensively.

I should know better than to try and slag off her best mate.

'Maybe you're right,' I begrudgingly agree with a shrug. 'Okay. Just between us.'

For now.

I lean down, cup her face and bring my lips to hers. How can this woman be so addictive and make me so stupid?

Chapter 11

Erica

Sunday

I wake up, my limbs sore from yesterday's shower session. Brooke's still passed out next to me so I check my phone. I have a text from a contact called Your Holiday Lover. A smile plasters itself onto my face. He's obviously got hold of my phone, the idiot. The sexy as hell idiot. I sigh like a love-struck teenager and open the message.

Morning. Can't sleep. Charlie is snoring his head off. I'm gonna ask Tom if he wants to swap with him. How you feeling today? x

I get such a ridiculous thrill from reading it. Why is it whenever I'm around him I turn into a giggling teenager? I really need to work on that. I decide to be a little cheeky with my reply.

A little sore ;-)

I watch as he views it. Then he's typing, the three dots taunting me. Holy moly, I need to get a grip.

Good. Will keep you thinking of me all day.

Swoon!

As if I wouldn't anyway...

Crap, that's made me sound like I'm obsessed with him. Damn, why did I get too click happy?

That's what I like to hear. Meet you at the bus for quad biking x

Crap, I forgot about that. Evelyn signed us up on the first day.

'Yeah, see you there.'

I look up from my phone and nearly jump out of my skin when I see Brooke awake and openly staring at me.

'Fuck! Brooke! You scared the shit out of me.'

She cackles. 'Well my sleeping self still recognised the typing of a phone. Who are you texting?'

I physically can't wipe the stupid grin off my face. Way to play it cool.

'Oh, just a friend back home.'

'Yeah right,' she laughs. 'You can't fool me. It's Jack, right?'

Shit, how does she know? Am I that pathetic?

'I'm not an idiot, Erica. Who else would be texting you the day after you got the fucking of your life!?' She throws back her head, chuckling hard.

I pout, a grin teasing at my lips. 'How do you know that I didn't give it to a local last night?'

She rolls her eyes. 'Please. You were passing each other these looks last night. The sexual tension was thick.'

'Okay, it's him,' I admit with a goofy grin.

Her face lights up. She rearranges herself into a comfortable sitting position, sensing the gossip like a dog smells out a sausage. 'Come on. I need details. I get that you don't want to scare Molly with all of the dick talk, but I want to know everything.'

I roll onto my side and remove some sleep out of my eyes. It's way too early to be talking about sex.

'Okay, well, he helped me with exfoliating and...'

'The feel of his hands on your body was too much, right?' she interrupts, her eyes light up excitedly. 'You fucked the life out of him, didn't you?' She smiles widely, practically bouncing up and down on the bed.

'It wasn't like that, actually,' I snap defensively. It wasn't. When I think back to it I can't help but remember it as magical. I mean, mindblowing and animalistic, yes. But it wasn't just some mindless fuck. It's as if I can still feel the tingling sensation on my skin as he touched me. 'It just...it just kind of happened,' I admit with a shrug. 'We ended up in the shower and before I knew what was happening we were having sex.'

'Ugh, that is *SO* hot.' She fans her face dramatically. 'What's his peen like?' She wiggles her eyebrows up and down.

I burst out laughing. I can't help it. When she gets this animated she's like a cartoon. Of course she only wants to know his dick size. Not what this means for us.

'He's okay...well, actually, he's huge,' I admit, with a smug smile. 'I always remember him having a really thin pencil dick, but my God, has he grown up.'

'Nice!' she claps. I can't help but think of a clapping seal.

Now's the time to confess to her. She's the only one I'm positive won't judge me.

'Yeah, only, it was so heat of the moment...we forgot to use a condom,' I admit, looking down into my lap.

'I'm sure he's clean,' she dismisses, as if it's no big deal. Her eyes suddenly widen as it dawns on her. 'Wait, didn't you recently come off the pill?'

'Exactly,' I nod, biting my thumb nail. 'I can't believe I've been so reckless. I need to get the morning after pill.'

'Oh my God,' she laughs, clapping her hands together. 'Evelyn is going to kill you!'

Trust her to find entertainment in my situation.

'I don't intend on telling her. And you'd better shut your mouth if you value your life.'

She snorts. 'As if! I need a roommate and if you're dead who's going to pay half the rent?'

I stare at her, eyebrows raised. 'I'm glad I mean that much to you,' I deadpan.

She cackles. She really is like a witch when it's just us and she's not giggling seductively in front of guys.

'And anyway, what went on with you and Tom? You didn't come back last night.' I heard her creep in at around three this morning.

She sighs, looking away listlessly. 'We fucked. Usual story.'

'And?' I ask eagerly, liking that the attention has been taken away from me. 'Still good?'

She groans. 'Too fucking good. I haven't been able to stop thinking about it.'

I study her face, trying to read her. This isn't like her. Normally she's a hit it and quit it type of girl. She doesn't have time for relationships.

'Normally when I have sex with them I get it out of my system, but with Tom...I don't know, it's like I just want more. I want it again. It's like he made his way under my skin or something.'

I grin at her. 'Sounds like someone has a crush,' I sing teasingly.

She picks up her pillow and throws it at me. 'As if! I'm a grown woman. I don't have crushes. But...well, what is it about the guys in Peterborough, eh? There must be something in the water.'

I crease up laughing. 'You are *too* hilarious! See, *this* is why I can tell you and not Evelyn.'

She nods in agreement. 'Yeah, remind me, why are you friends with her again?' She's smiling, but I can tell it's a serious question.

Brooke and Evelyn have never really got on like a house on fire. She thinks she's too serious and Evelyn thinks Brooke is too wild. You probably couldn't get further ends of the spectrum.

'Because I've known her all my life and can trust her with anything. I don't think I know a single person better on this planet.'

'Just because you've known her forever, doesn't mean you've not outgrown her,' she counters.

'Hey! Look, I might chat shit about her to you now and again, but you know I love her and won't have a bad word said against her.'

'Ok,' she sighs, rolling her eyes. 'Whatever you say.' She jumps out of bed and stretches, her bare breasts stuck in my face. I roll so I'm face down on the bed.

'Dude! I really wish you'd wear pyjamas.'

She laughs and smacks my butt. 'Come on you little slut. We've got a morning after pill to hunt down.'

Excess BAGGAGE

'I just don't understand,' Evelyn says over breakfast. Trust her to be up this early. We were hoping we could sneak out without anyone seeing us. 'Why can't you just come on the bus to quad biking with the rest of us?'

I can feel my cheeks burning. 'It's no big deal, okay. We just want to have a bit more of a sleep and we'll get a cab over later.'

'You look perfectly well slept to me.' She turns to Brooke. 'Come on Brooke, surely you have more stamina than this? We've not even had any wild benders yet.'

'Yeah, well we deserve some rest all the same,' Brooke says with a sweet smile, glancing a look at me. I'm surprised she's being so well behaved. Actually, no I'm not. I threatened to burn her Tom Hardy calendar if she didn't.

Evelyn looks between the both of us. 'Okay, cut the crap. What's going on? Where are you really going?'

Shit, she's onto us. My stomach starts contracting in panic while I try to think of something. But hell, I can't think of *one* valid excuse. I look to Brooke helplessly, my cheeks on fire. She widens her eyes discreetly, clearly also drawing a blank.

'I...' I murmur, unsure how I'm going to get out of this. With Evelyn's calculating stare focusing in on me it's harder to think straight. It's like bloody laser beams, burning away any sensible thoughts.

Brooke winks at me. It doesn't fill me with confidence.

'I'm getting the morning after pill,' she explains boldly. She leans back in her chair, no doubt waiting for a berating from Evelyn.

My heart swells with warmth for her. I can't believe she took the bullet for me. Now *that's* a good friend.

'WHAT?' she exclaims, so loudly the whole eating hall quietens and turns to look at us. I hate when she goes into teacher mode.

I widen my eyes at Evelyn accusingly. 'Shut up, Evelyn!' I whisper hiss.

'I'm sorry,' she whispers back, looking around and noticing others staring, 'but how on earth could you be so irresponsible Brooke? I mean, I know you sleep around, but I thought you were at least careful. I mean, who is the guy? He could have STD's for all you know. Do you even know how chlamydia can affect your fertility long term? I mean, you could never be able to have children.'

'Whoa!' Brooke interrupts with her hands up in surrender. 'Yeah, it was a fuck up. But it's done now. I just need to get it sorted and Erica's offered to hold my hand.'

'Are you sure you don't need me to come with you

too?' she asks seriously. Bless her; judging one minute and concerned the next.

'I'm sure,' she nods with an eye roll.

'Who was it anyway?' Brooke looks to me in question.

'It was Tom!' I blurt quickly. Shit, why did I lay the blame at Tom? It's Evelyn. She puts me too much on edge.

'Tom!' she repeats loudly in horror.

'Someone say my name?'

We all turn to see Tom and Jack looking down at us. Shit, how long have they been standing there?

Evelyn glares at him. 'Yes, we might have been talking about you,' she snaps, glaring at him with disdain. 'But don't get a big head. It wasn't complimentary.'

He frowns down at us in bewilderment. 'Err...okay?'

Brooke pulls a grimace, as if trying to communicate that she's sorry. Not that she can tell him what she's sorry for without giving me up.

'So...' Tom says, looking between us all in confusion. 'Will we see you guys at quad biking?'

'Not us,' I say with a head shake. 'But Evelyn is going.'

Evelyn is basically growling at Tom, her upper lip quivering with rage. That girl really stands up for her girlfriends, even if she is a nutter.

'Not that I'll be anywhere near *you*, pretty boy,' she snaps, whipping her head back to look at her breakfast.

Jack raises his eyebrows in question at me. I give a non-committal shrug.

'Okay...well...we'll see you later, then.'

Chapter 12

Erica

'Brooke, I am *so* sorry you had to put up with that. Thank you so much for taking the hit.'

'Ah, it's fine,' she dismisses with a wave of her hand. 'Now we've just got to find the nearest chemist.'

See, this right here is how I could tell her. She's such a good friend. Just willing to help me without attempting to give me a lecture. We make our way up to the holiday rep who looks no older than twenty.

'Hello ladies, how can I help you?' he asks, with a professional smile.

'Err...' I look to Brooke. 'We need to find a local chemist.'

He nods. 'Ah, well you're in luck. The hotel carries paracetamol and aspirin, for sale at reception.'

He turns, as if to dismiss us, looking back down at his clipboard. Like pool Zumba is more important. I look to Brooke for help.

'No,' she insists, 'you don't understand. We need some proper medication. It's kind of a private issue.'

'Oh, okay,' he says, eyeing us suspiciously. 'Well there's one at the other side of the island. You can get a taxi for fifty euros or take three buses for ten.'

I look to Brooke. There's no way we have that kind of money for a taxi.

'Bus it is then,' I smile grimly.

'Okay. Let me write down the directions for you.'

After two hours of sweaty buses and getting lost because that guy has worse handwriting than a doctor, we're finally here.

'This is it?' Brooke asks, looking up at the shack like building.

It looks like it's been crafted from thick mud, its roof made from straw.

'Apparently.' I mean, it does have a red cross outside of it.

We walk in, surprised to find it's set out just like a normal chemist. I was half expecting to find a woman crushing up herbs on the floor. We scan over all of the foreign written labels. Crap, we're gonna have to ask. I'm sure it's an over the counter kind of thing anyway.

'I sure hope they stock the bloody thing,' I whisper in her ear.

She laughs, like this is no big deal. Like we didn't just trek halfway across the island to be here to ensure I don't get pregnant.

I walk up to the woman behind the counter and smile wildly. Please speak English, please speak English.

'Hi!' The woman looks back at me, no expression on her face. 'Do you...speak English?'

She waves her hand about. 'Little.'

'Great!' Brooke says, sighing in relief.

I smile, finally feeling positive. 'Okay, I need the morning after pill please.'

The woman looks back at me blankly. Well, she obviously speaks VERY little English.

'Morning after pill?' I repeat.

She shakes her hand again. 'Little.'

Fuck. I'm guessing that's the only English word she knows. I look to Brooke. I'm going to have to act this out.

I start cradling a pretend baby. 'Morning after pill,' I say again. I pretend to drop the baby and shake my hands away as if to show that I don't want the baby.

'Ah.'

Thank God, she gets me. She leans under the counter and produces a small box. I pick it up. It's foreign but I can see from the pictures that its plasters. Damn.

'No.' I shake my head. 'Morning after pill.' I do the baby cradle thing again, then shake my head and point to my right.

'Ah.' She produces what looks like children's calpol.

Okay, I'm clearly having no luck with the whole baby thing. Instead I start gyrating my hips against Brooke, pretending to have sex with her. The woman looks even more confused. I spin a giggling Brooke round and pretend to take her from behind. She shakes her head about as if it's real.

'Ah.' This time we get condoms.

I sigh heavily. Okay, we're getting close. I pretend to shag Brooke, then point wildly to the right and then cradle my arms like I have a baby. Then shake my head. I'm sweating now. Please God she'll get it this time.

'Ah! Ah!' She seems excited.

'Yes!'

She grabs a phone and calls someone speaking wildly in her language. I'm sure even if I spoke the language I wouldn't be able to cotton on to what she's on about. Within a minute another guy runs into the chemist, speaking to her. She gestures wildly at us.

'Come on,' he says in broken English. He grabs us and drags us out to his jeep.

'Wait, where are you taking us?'

Is he trying to kidnap us so that we can be sold as sex

slaves?

'To your hotel,' he answers. 'To deliver the baby.'

Brooke bursts out laughing. I groan. 'No, there is no baby. I just need the morning after pill.'

He stops in his tracks. 'Oh. Oh, very different.'

He takes us back in the chemist and speaks with the lady behind the counter. She looks at us as if we're filthy animals. I suppose they don't get many people asking for morning after pills here. She begrudgingly hands over a box with two tablets.

The doctor explains how it should be taken.

'Thank you so much,' I say, my cheeks practically puce. 'I'm not normally like this. Not this kind of girl. You see, he's my first love and... well, it just kind of-'

'He doesn't care, Erica,' Brooke laughs. 'But are you going back inland? We could use a lift?'

The lovely man dropped us at the quad biking as it was actually closer than the hotel. We thank him and make our way over to the instructors.

'Now remember what I said, Brooke,' I warn, 'you have to help me hide it.'

'And like I told *you*, you need to ride on anyone but Jack's quad bike. Understood?'

Dammit, I know she's right, but it doesn't mean I'm

not already mourning the feel of my arms around his waist. Any excuse to touch him sounds great, but she's right. Evelyn will sniff it out like a greyhound.

We introduce ourselves to the English woman running it.

'Your friends are over there,' she explains, pointing far off somewhere. 'We can radio some back so you can jump on the back of theirs if you like?'

'Yeah, that would be great,' I nod, already letting the nerves get the better of me.

'Get Jack and Tom for us, will you?'

Jack

Our quad biking tour guide pulls over, gesturing for me and Tom to follow him.

'We need to go back,' he shouts through his helmet. 'Your other friends have arrived.'

Ah Erica's finally arrived from wherever the hell she's been. It's crazy but I've missed her. How pathetic is that!

We follow him back to the starting track. As soon as we've pulled over I yank my helmet eye screen up so I can take her in. Is it crazy that she looks hotter than this morning? I really need to pull myself together. She's only been away a few hours. I wink at her. She smiles back, clearly swooning.

I wait for her to jump on my quad bike but she seems to be walking towards Tom. What the hell? She takes a helmet held out by the instructor and jumps on, clinging onto his back.

What. The. Actual. Fuck?

Brooke jumps onto mine, but I can't acknowledge her. I'm too fucking confused and pissed off with Erica. She looks back, appearing apologetic before Tom zooms off. With my bloody woman.

Brooke wraps her arms around my waist. 'Come on cowboy. Let's ride!'

I roll my eyes and race after them. Wherever they're going I'm following. I don't want to give Tom a chance to try it on with her. This morning I was sure she'd turn him down. Now I'm not so sure.

We race through the wildlife, burnt rusty roads whizzing past us. He finally slows down and eventually stops. Shit, we've done the track already. I've been so focused on them I haven't noticed.

'Whoo!' Brooke screams, kicking her legs up in the air. 'That was amazing, right? Oh my God, the views!'

I ignore her, too busy watching as Tom swings his leg off the bike. I quickly take my helmet off so I can hear what he's saying.

'How was that gorgeous? You have the ride of your life? he says, with a wink.

She rolls her eyes. 'I won't be repeating it, that's for sure,' she drawls sarcastically.

I smile, glad she's rebuffing his advances. That's got to mean something. Right?

Brooke runs off to the others, obviously sick of me ignoring her. Tom holds out his hand for her to get off. She places her shaky hand in his.

'Wow, you really didn't enjoy it, did you?' he grins.

She swings her leg over and climbs off. 'You can say that again.'

'Oh wait.' He looks down to the floor. 'Something fell out of your pocket.' He bends down to pick something up.

I can't see it. I didn't think she'd dropped anything. She checks her pockets. Her face suddenly pales.

He picks something up and looks back up at her. 'What's this?'

'It's nothing,' she says, attempting to grab it off him. He holds it higher.

'It doesn't sound like nothing.'

I shake my head. Tom can be a nosy prick sometimes.

'Leave her alone, Tom,' I snap, snatching the box from him.

She looks even more nervous now, a sheen of barely there sweat on her forehead. Why is she being so weird around me?

I glance down at it, nosy bastard that I am and go to hand it back before snatching it back and having a closer look, my eyebrows narrowed in concentration.

'Morning after pill?' I read out loud, dumbfounded.

She squirms under my intense stare. Morning after pill. As in she's not on the pill? What the hell?

'No way!' Tom giggles. 'Get you, you little dark horse.'

'It's mine actually,' Brooke says, snatching them from my hand.

Oh, thank fuck for that. I've never been more relieved.

Tom's face falls. 'What? What the fuck are you talking about Brooke? We used a johnny. Didn't we?' His eyes widen. 'Shit, didn't we?'

'What makes you think it's even for you?' she asks cockily, hand on her jut out hip.

Ouch. That's gotta hurt his self-esteem.

'Nice,' he grunts. 'Real nice Brooke.'

'Oh, so it's okay for you to sleep around, but just because I'm a woman I'm a slut?'

They start going at each other, but I'm too busy watching Erica curiously. I take her hand and pull her away from them.

I know Erica too well. It's hers. The way she can barely meet my gaze tells me everything she can't say.

'It's yours, isn't it?' I ask, letting go of her hand.

She goes red, tucking a bit of hair behind her ear as she stares at my trainers. 'Um...'

'For fuck's sake, Eric,' I sigh. 'I assumed you were on the pill.'

How could she not tell me? Something so important like this? And more worryingly, how could I not have double-checked with her. I know fucking better.

She rolls her eyes, suddenly seeming defensive. 'I don't remember you stopping to ask any questions.'

She's right.

'Yeah, well you should have stopped me. Why didn't you?'

She sighs heavily. 'I guess I got carried away in the moment, just like you. If I remember, it wasn't exactly planned.'

She's right. 'Yeah I suppose. So, have you taken it?'

'Taken the first pill. I need to take the second one in twelve hours.'

'Okay.' I nod, my eyes creased in worry. 'Just make sure you remember.'

'Don't worry, Jack,' she scoffs with an eye roll. 'I'm not trying to get pregnant.' She crosses her arms over her chest and walks off towards the others.

'Eric!' I call after her. A few people turn round. Shit, I'm drawing attention to us. I chance a worried smile her way.

She smiles sadly back. She might as well have gutted me with a hook. She turns away from me. Shit. Well I've completely fucked this up.

Chapter 13

Erica

I still can't believe he reacted like that. I know it must have been a shock, but bloody hell, no need to freak out quite so much. It's not like I sent him a devastating text that'll haunt him for fifteen years. No, that was him. Well I don't care how much Jack apologises tonight; he's not getting back into my pants on this holiday. He can beg me for all I care.

My door knocks. I bet it's Jack trying to start his grovelling.

'Brooke, can you get it?' I shout from the bathroom, still doing my make-up. I want to look extra hot tonight so I can feel confident when I tell him to go to hell.

I hear the door open and muffled voices.

'Erica, I think you're gonna want to see this,' Brooke calls through to me.

A thrill travels through me. Has he turned up

dressed in a tuxedo with a dozen roses? I know that's far-fetched, but he must have done something interesting for her to be talking like that.

I turn on my heel and skip out, ready to tear him a new one. Only, instead of him it's Karl. Dumped over an email fucking Karl! I stand motionless, staring at him, my mouth practically touching the floor.

'What the hell are you doing here?'

He smiles. 'Surprise!'

He's fucking telling me.

His face falls when I don't run over and fling myself into his arms. What the hell is going on? Did he not get my email? I'm sure I pressed send. Didn't I? Oh Jesus, I feel sick at the thought of him having not read it yet.

'Karl.' It's all I can say.

His face falls. 'Aren't you glad to see me?'

He can't have got the email. Holy fuck, the guy thinks we're still together. Meanwhile I've fucked Jack. Jesus, that means I'm an adulterer.

'No, err...of course I am!'

Brooke looks at me, her eyes raised so high they're practically in her hairline.

'It's just...err, we were on our way out. I thought you were one of the girls.'

'Well, I don't want to stop you.' Bless him, never wanting to put anyone out. 'I'll come with.'

Oh shit. I don't want him bumping into Jack. He doesn't even know about him!

'Really?' I shrill, clear panic in my voice. 'Why don't you chill out here for a while? You must be knackered after that long flight.'

'No, I'd really like to come with you,' he smiles, taking my hand. It feels so foreign in mine. 'I fancy a cocktail right about now.' Has he always been this camp?

Shit.

'Oh...okay.'

He turns, heading for the door. Brooke's eyes nearly gouge out of their sockets, clearly panicking on my behalf. I can do nothing more than stare back at her, grimacing in dread.

The whole walk there I'm looking over my shoulder, expecting to see Jack at any minute. I have no idea what the hell I'm going to say. I mean, I managed to pull my hand out of Karl's, claiming sweaty hands, but he keeps trying to take hold of it again. How the heck am I going to explain this?

There I was worrying about Jack being an arsehole and I'm the one who's had their boyfriend turn up on the same holiday. The boyfriend I'm pretty sure I dumped. Damn it, that's karmas way of telling me off for trying to break up with someone over email.

We walk towards the others, already waiting in a

group at reception. I can already see Jack, laughing along to something Charlie's said. Crap, this is going to be awful. I feel like a balloon animal, knotted and twisted up in all the wrong places.

Molly's the first one to see us. She waves wildly, before her hand falls down and her face pales. They all seem to turn at the same time, their faces priceless. The girls take one look at Karl and their eyes widen in horror. They look to me, their eyebrows raised in a mix of shock and pity. Brooke's trying to signal something behind me but I can't make out what.

The guys look him over suspiciously, obviously wondering where the hell he's come from. Maybe they think I picked him up earlier. I've avoided looking at Jack the entire time, but I know I can't avoid it forever.

I steel myself and take a deep breath before allowing myself to look up and at him. Jack's cheeks have actually turned red, and he's staring intently at Karl. His gaze finds mine and the hurt and confusion in it is too much. I have to look away.

'Who's this?' Tom asks, pointing to him.

I have no idea how I'm going to explain this without looking like a massive slaggy whore.

'This is Karl,' Brooke says for me. I smile gratefully at her.

Karl offers his hand out to shake Tom's. 'Erica's

boyfriend,' he announces proudly. 'Nice to meet you.'

And just like that I feel guilt and shame take over my body, strangling me to death. I can't look at Jack. I just can't. I'm a monster. A reckless little slut.

I must completely black out or something because when I manage to refocus we've started to walk.

'You okay?' Karl asks, taking my hand.

I look up to see Jack staring at our linked hands. This is fucking awful. I can't break his hand without him thinking something is up and right now I have no idea what to do. I need to take him off somewhere private and explain that we're not working anymore. Tell him what I wrote in the email.

Only...well I'm a big fat chicken shit, aren't I? That's why I sent an email in the first fucking place. I can't just shout to him that it's over. Not when he's been through so much with me.

We go into our usual bar and get drinks. I see Jack make his way towards the toilets and quickly follow behind him. I wait until he comes out, tapping my foot nervously. He walks out, spotting me, his eyes widening, before quickly trying to walk around me.

'Jack, please!' I call, pulling on his arm. 'Listen to me.'

'Listen to what?' he shouts, throwing his arm out of my reach. 'How you've had a fucking boyfriend this entire time?' His nostrils flare. I've never seen them do that before. For a second I want to giggle, but I quickly pull myself together.

'No, it's not like that! Well, it was, but then...'

'I can't believe you,' he interrupts, a vein becoming engorged on his neck. 'I suppose it's my own fault for putting you on a pedestal all these years, but I thought you were different. Now within twenty four hours I find we've had unprotected sex without my knowledge and now you have a fucking boyfriend! Who looks like a right plank, by the way.'

'I dumped him!' I shout over him. 'I dumped him almost as soon as I saw you. Before we had sex. But...well, he's just turned up here and I don't know if he's even got my email.'

'Email?' He narrows his eyes. 'You dumped the guy, over fucking *email?*'

'Err...yeah,' I admit with an awkward shrug. I suppose that doesn't put me in a better light, really.

He runs his hands through his hair, his eyes tight. 'Jesus, Erica. Just when I think you can't shock me more.'

I can already feel him pulling away from me, not physically, but emotionally. Any trust I'd built up with him has well and truly jumped off a cliff.

'Please Jack, listen to me,' I plead, holding onto his bicep. I feel like if I let go I'm going to lose him forever.

'Why the fuck should I?' he yells, throwing my arm off again. 'I don't see you telling that guy out there to fuck off and go home. What's he doing here anyway? Interrupting a girl's holiday?' He scoffs. 'Screams jealous and possessive to me.'

'I don't know...I just...god, everything is such a mess.' I have a migraine the size of Canada lurking.

'You're telling me,' he scoffs. He turns and storms out, leaving me no choice but to follow him. But the minute I'm out Karl is grabbing my arm and pulling me to one side.

'Erica, we need to talk.'

Oh, thank goodness. He's seen the chemistry between me and Jack and has realised it's over between us.

'Yes, you're right, we need to.' I steel myself to be horrible. It needs to be done, but it still doesn't stop me feeling like a giant bitch.

'I got your email.'

He GOT it? Then why the fuck is he here? I'm so confused right now, it's as if my thoughts are whirling around inside my head like a tornado.

'I've been thinking about it and you're right,' he continues. Wait, so he agrees we should split up? Thank God. That's going to make things a whole lot easier. 'We *have* been drifting apart and we've been under a lot of stress because of your mum, so it's given me the kick up the arse I needed.'

"Kick up the arse?" What the hell is he talking about?

'So...' He reaches into his pocket and then falls to the floor. No wait, he hasn't fallen, he's landed on one knee. No, he isn't...no. No? No, no, *no*.

'Will you marry me, Erica?'

He opens a red velvet box to show a tiny diamond so underwhelming I actually gasp in horror.

I look around to see that everyone in the bar is staring. Everyone including Jack. He looks crestfallen, all colour drained from his face. He turns and leaves, banging the main door shut behind him. Tom gives me a disapproving look before running out after him.

I look down at Karl, grinning up at me in excitement. Can he really be that dumb?

'Well...' he beams, seeming completely hopeful, 'what's your answer?'

'Err...no.'

Chapter 14

Monday

Erica

Well what a fucking disaster last night was. After humiliating Karl like that in front of everyone, I had to take him outside and explain to him how I've been feeling like this for a long time, and that meant admitting to subconsciously using him through my mum's chemo. It was awful. I could tell he was angry but being Karl, he told me he understood. He even admitted that he'd been fooling himself thinking that I'd say yes to his proposal, but felt he had to try.

He got a cab straight to the airport to try to get an earlier flight. He could still be there for all I know. Brooke keeps telling me not to worry, that he willingly wasted his money on the off- chance I'd say yes. Doesn't stop me feeling bad though.

What makes me feel even worse is that I was far more bothered about where Jack ran off to. Knowing he hadn't got the full story from me had my heart aching. I tried to call him all night but he kept ignoring my calls. I even got Tom's number from Charlie and tried to call him but it was turned off. I ended up drinking myself silly and trying to break into their hotel room. He clearly wasn't back yet. Pretty sure he'd have answered the door to a drunken woman trying to beat down his door.

It's sad to say but I missed Jack last night. So much. The minute I opened my eyes I knew I had to see him. Anyway, now that I've had my breakfast I'm ready to speak to him. I need him to see how badly I've fallen for him.

Now, today he won't have a chance to get away from me. We've all booked to go on this boat trip around the island to snorkle so I'm going to be stuck with his confrontation. Ugh, I can't be bothered. See, this is why I'm single. I just can't be arsed with drama.

I spot him the minute we arrive at reception. Why is it he looks even more beautiful now that I've screwed up any chance with him? Damn that tan is working for him.

We get ushered onto the bus. I follow the girls to the back and sit in a seat in the second to the back row, staring out of the window. Anything to stop me from staring at him. I hate that I'm pining like a teenager, but my god, all of this time without him near me has caused my heart to ache. I want his body near me more than I need my next breath.

The seat shifts underneath me. I look around to see Tom has sat next to me, but is turned to chat to the girls behind. That suits me fine. Well, until Jack sits down in front of me.

His being so close is doing something stupid to me. The desperation to clear the air is stronger than any self respect I'm clinging onto. I pat him on the shoulder, forcing him to turn round to face me.

'So, are you going to talk to me at all for the rest of the holiday?' I ask, sounding a lot more confident than I feel. I can't help but smile at him, when I should be doing anything but. Damn it, why does he have to be so cute?

'Dammit, you're annoying,' he says back to me with an irritated smile.

'I have loads to tell you.' I look around to make sure the others aren't listening. Luckily Charlie's entertaining them with some story. 'Look, I'm sorry that I didn't tell you I was with someone at the start of the holiday, but in my defence, I didn't think I was going to bump into you after fifteen years.'

He nods, his lips tight. 'I suppose I can understand that.'

'But I broke up with him. First by email and then

again last night. He gets it now. He's on his way back home.'

He sighs, his eyes weary. 'Don't break up with him because of me, Erica.'

'Why not?' I can't help but ask, like a desperate girl. Does that mean he's not offering me anything? That this is just a bit of meaningless fun? Which I suppose of course it is. It's not like I can expect for this to continue into real life when we get home.

'Because this isn't going anywhere,' he shrugs. 'We both know after this week we have to go back to our own lives and that means living in different postcodes. It would never work.'

Well, yeah, if he has that defeatist attitude and doesn't even want to try! I mean, is it too much to ask for a guy to fight for me a bit? Karl was jumping on a plane and flying miles across the world just on the off-chance I'd give him another chance. And here Jack is giving up before anything's even started properly.

'So, what exactly are you saying?' I ask, gulping down the unshed tears that are threatening to spill. Why am I so emotional? I knew this wasn't going to last, so why am I feeling so upset? I suppose I was clinging onto the thought of being with him until we left. The thought of being this close to him but being unable to touch him feels soul destroying.

He rubs the back of his neck. 'I'm saying that maybe you should rethink his proposal.'

My mouth drops open of its own accord. I can't believe what he's saying. That I should marry Karl. What the hell? Why do I feel so shocked and devastated? We've never established what we mean to each other while on this holiday. Yes, we shagged, he got pissed off when he thought I was trying it on with other men, but then we agreed to keep it a secret. For all I know he was just happy to have a holiday bunk up buddy. I could have been any girl on this bus. I'm not special to him at all. I've been fooling myself this whole time.

But...well, the way he looks at me, like right now, with the look of wonder in his eyes whenever I catch him staring at me. Well, it gives me hope. It's stupid to have hope, I know. It's not like we could ever be anything past this holiday, but it doesn't stop me fantasizing about a happily ever after with him. One where we live in the same place and destiny has finally aligned for us to be together. It's stupid. I'm being so foolish.

I turn away from him, deciding instead to stare out of the window. Do not cry, Erica, do *not* cry.

We steal stupid glances at each other the whole way there, blushing and smiling bashfully whenever we're caught by the other. Now and again Tom tries to include me in the conversation with the girls, but he quickly cops on that I'm not in the mood. I tell him I'm sleepy. That all the partying has done me in. Not the truth, that I'm heartbroken.

When we arrive, a tubby Spaniard man greets us and hands out disclaimers for us to sign. Slightly alarming.

'Sorry, but why do we have to sign these?' I ask, fear creeping up my neck and wrapping itself around me. I've never actually been on a boat, but I'm assuming these butterflies will calm down as soon as I'm aboard.

'Just in case,' he smiles, with a dismissing wave.

'Yeah, chill out Erica,' Brooke laughs. 'We're hardly going to die. It's just a boat trip.'

'I bet that's what the passengers of the titanic said too,' Alice adds, hugging herself around the stomach. I must pale because she quickly adds, 'but I'm sure this is totally safe.'

Scenes from Titanic flash through my mind. Shit, what if it does sink?

'Are there any sharks around here?' Molly asks innocently, scratching at her neck.

'You *can't* be serious,' Evelyn snaps, rising her eyebrows at her.

'What?' she giggles. 'They were in Devon! If they can get to Devon they can get to Luna Island.'

'No worry,' the man says with a chuckle. 'No sharks here. Just beautiful sea to snorkle in.'

I take a look at Molly. We both said last night that we're not keen on the idea of snorkelling. I mean, I actually have a severe fear of wearing goggles. Don't ask me why, but the minute I go under the water I somehow panic and think I'm drowning. There's no rationality behind it. So, imagine me with one of those things in my mouth! I'd probably have a panic attack and be found floating around dead like a mauled turtle.

Everyone starts using the small ledge to climb onto the modest, white boat. Looks safe enough I suppose. There are rows of seats we can sit on or we can just wander round. I choose the seats. At least that way I'll feel grounded.

'In just twenty minutes we'll be at our destination, so sit back, relax and enjoy the scenery,' the tubby man says cheerfully.

The boats engine starts whirring loudly and then we're off. I hold on a bit too tightly to the bar in front of me. Damn, I hate not being on land. I'm the same with planes - anything where I'm not in control really. It makes me nervous. Ugh, and this boat is rocking from side to side so deep I feel as if we're going to fall over the side.

My stomach starts contracting in fear, feeling heavy as lead, and I begin to feel nauseous.

'Are you okay, babe?' Alice asks, looking at me

worriedly.

'I feel a bit...' The motion of going from left to right is making me want to hug the floor. 'A bit...'

'Shit,' Evelyn says, turning and spotting me. 'Erica, you look fucking green! Are you going to chuck up?'

I hope Jack's at the other end of the boat with the rest of the guys and didn't just hear that.

'I...' I swallow down some bile that's attempting to rise from my throat. 'I think I might.' I try to calm myself down by taking some deep breaths, but it's no use. If anything I'm feeling sicker.

'Oh, gosh almighty,' Molly squeals. 'If she gets sick, *I'll* get sick!'

Evelyn rolls her eyes. 'It's fine. I'll take her.'

She puts her arm around my waist and helps me up. It's times like this I love her more than anything. She's going to make an amazing mum one day.

She guides me towards the side of the boat. It's hard to even walk on this thing with it throwing us from side to side. I hold onto the rail and look over the side into the ocean. My God, this is making me feel even worse. I collapse down onto my knees, wanting to be close to the floor. When the boat tips this way it feels like I might fall over into the water. Woman overboard! I still think it would feel better than being on this boat. Unless Molly's right and there are sharks.

I vomit, the velocity taking me by surprise. Evelyn holds my hair back like a best friend should and allows me to chuck my guts up over the side. I throw up until my stomach is empty yet I'm still gagging. Just in time for the boat to slowly stop. An anchor is thrown overboard.

Everyone starts to strip down to their bikinis, the man handing out snorkels at the other end of the boat. There's no way I'm snorkelling now.

I lay on my back while Alice passes me some wet tissue to put on my forehead.

'You'll be okay, hun,' Evelyn soothes, pushing my hair back off my face.

The sun blasts down on my face, making me feel even sicker. There's nothing worse than having to sweat like this while you're vomiting up breakfast.

'Shit.' I turn my head slightly to follow the voice and find Jack leaning over me, his shadow shielding me from the relentless rays. 'What happened?'

I go to open my mouth, but it's so dry, I decide not to bother.

'She's seasick, *obviously*,' Evelyn snaps, rolling her eyes irritably.

He sighs, leaning on one hip. 'I can see that,' he snaps back. 'How long has she been chucking up?'

Why is he pretending he even cares?

'Over twenty minutes,' Evelyn answers, without

giving him any eye contact.

'Shit, should we speak to the captain?'

'And what?' she practically snarls. 'Ask him to stop everyone snorkelling so we can bring the one sick passenger back to shore? Or should I tell him when we do get going to go fast? Risk the lives of the rest of us just so we can get there a bit quicker?'

She's such a sarcastic cow.

He sighs, as if defeated. 'Whatever. There's no reason to be such a dick to me.'

Oh God, I could really do without them arguing right now. I don't have the energy to break them apart.

'Whatever,' she snorts, shaking her head as if she's talking to an intolerable toddler.

'Why don't you go off and enjoy the rest of the ride and I'll look after her,' he suggests.

Why on earth would he do that? He just told me to marry Karl. He doesn't give a shit about me.

'You certainly will not!' she rebuffs with a cruel laugh.

He scoffs, gritting his teeth. 'Yes, I will.'

'Paha! Coming from the guy that left her broken-hearted and crying on my shoulder all those years ago. Call me silly but I'd say I'm better equipped at looking after her than you are.'

Jack looks at me with furrowed brows, hurt radiating

from his pores. 'Erica, are you going to let her talk to me like this?'

I shrug, having no energy to do anything else. 'Too ill to fight,' I croak, my throat burning from the attempt.

'Yeah, just go,' Evelyn snaps cruelly.

He crouches down, close to my face. His scent is welcome after just smelling vomit for the last twenty minutes.

'Erica, tell Evelyn that I mean something to you. That I should be allowed to stay and help look after you.' He strokes the hair off my forehead. It feels heavenly.

I gaze up into his concerned deep hazel eyes and want nothing more than to ask him to stay. But to admit that would be to admit that I still have feelings for him. Something I've denied to Evelyn. Something he denied himself less than thirty minutes ago. If she sniffs out this holiday fling she'll lock me in my room and leave me there till the flight is departing. I only have one option.

'You should go,' I mutter, giving him a weak smile.

The hurt twists his face. Evelyn looks sickeningly happy about it. I feel the guilt wrap its way around my intestines. Or is that just another dose of sickness? Who knows? I only know that I've made a mistake as he begrudgingly backs away from me, running his hand through his hair, his face twisted with hurt.

What the hell have I done?

Chapter 15

Jack

I can't believe she dissed me like that. And in front of Evelyn too. That bitch has never liked me. Even from way before we split up. Never trusted me. It's not fair. I get that she was ill, but would it have really hurt to just say I could help look after her?

Shit, when I saw her laid out like that I nearly had a heart attack. All I wanted to do was gather her small body up in my arms and hold her to my chest until she felt better. I'd only ever feel like that for Erica. I used to hate when girlfriends got sick and would stay away at all costs. With her I can't help but feel protective over her. I want her to be mine to look after.

When did I get so pussy whipped? Actually, I can pinpoint it back to when I was sixteen. She's always been different to other girls. Special. Maybe it's because she was my first love. Not that I think I loved her; but at that age everything is a lustful all-consuming fascination, isn't it? Every morning I woke up I couldn't wait to speak to her and now those feelings are creeping back.

That's why I've stopped it before it gets out of hand. I mean, she wanted to keep us a secret. Embarrassed to admit she's with me. All because she had a boyfriend back home. I can't believe she didn't tell me. Seeing him with her last night shocked the fuck out of me. And when that little fucker went down on one knee to propose I just had to get out of there.

It made me doubt her. Maybe she's no longer the innocent Erica I remember, but a calculating, manipulating older version. Maybe she's just like the rest of them.

I must have kicked over three bins on the walk back. When she tried to bang on my door, begging to explain I knew that I couldn't answer it. I was too mad. Instead I had a shower to try to drown out the noise.

I barely got any sleep all night thinking about it. What the hell did I have to offer her anyway? It's not like I could move up her way and we know from past experience that long distance doesn't work. And I wouldn't want it to. If I was with her, I'd want to be with her properly, waking up to her every morning.

So, I've decided to let her go. Told her she should reconsider that tools proposal. I'm going to desperately try to forget her and have the fun on this holiday that I thought I would. I'm growing back my pair of balls and taking back hold of this holiday.

Erica

I feel soooooo much better! My God am I a land bird. I've had a shower and a nap so I'm feeling good as new. I apply my lipstick and think about how I'm going to apologise to Jack later. I can't get his sad, dejected face out of my mind. Every time I see it it's as if someone stabs me in the heart. It's affected me far worse than Karl's.

I've decided that as soon as the others relax into drinking I'll pull him aside and apologise. Tonight, we're going on the excursion bus to the one club on the island. Apparently it's their two-for-one cocktails, which I think is as wild as it gets around here. Brooke tells me the guys took an earlier taxi, impatient bastards.

I can't help but miss the guys not being with us. It's sad to think we've come to rely on them in this short time, but they're fun to have around. We load onto the bus for the twenty minute journey.

Some old lady in front of us takes forever getting out of her seat and walking down the steps. Why the hell is she coming out to a bar in the first place? By the time we make it into the club I spot them by the bar surrounded by a gaggle of blonde, big-titted bimbos. Boys will be boys I suppose.

This club is actually adorable. It's only slightly larger than our local bar and is full of old-fashioned looking mahogany furniture. They've stapled things to the walls and ceiling like they do in TGIF's, maybe to hide cracks in the old walls. They've tried to jazz it up a bit by having neon lights behind the bar and a small DJ booth in the corner. The DJ is blaring out Rockabye by Sean Paul and Clean Bandit.

But then I see that Jack is flirting away, making two blondes in particular laugh their arses off, tits jumping up and down in their tops, threatening to spill over. He can't stop looking at them as they bounce either. What the fuck? What is he playing at?

'Ignore it, babe,' Brooke says, a hand on my shoulder. 'He's just trying to get a reaction.'

'Well, he's getting one,' I begrudgingly admit.

'Let's just stop being girls for tonight and do some shots,' Alice says, a mischievous look in her eyes. 'Dance like Beyoncé. Forget all about stinky boys.'

'I'll cheer to that.'

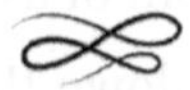

So, a few hours later I'm a bit more pissed and I'm

also feeling a bit braver. The girls are right; dancing to Beyoncé's *Run the World (girls)* does empower you. And now I'm feeling angry. Really fucking angry. How dare this little prick ignore me like this! He has no right to try and play with my emotions like that. Yeah, I upset him earlier, but if he'd have given me half a second I'd have had a chance to apologise. Instead he chose to push those big-titted blondes in my face. Well fuck him!

I charge over to him, feeling every emotion rising from my gut into words I'm desperate to spill at him. I push past the two bimbos and charge at him. His eyes widen in alarm.

'You!' I practically shout. I grab his arm and start dragging him towards the exit. I'm shocking myself how strong I am right now. He trails on behind me.

'What's going on Erica? Stop!'

I get him out of the door and up the steps towards the coach, then turn and stick my finger into his chest.

'Ow! Eric, what the fuck?'

'Err, no. You don't get the cheek to ask me what the fuck is happening! What the fuck do YOU think you're doing blatantly flirting with those bitches right in front of me?'

He scoffs, putting his hands in his pockets. 'Well, call me stupid, but I remember clearly asking you if you felt anything for me earlier and you told me to go away.'

'Yes, in front of Evelyn! I was obviously going to apologise as soon as I got a chance to speak to you, but now you've just proved Evelyn's point by acting like a man-whore. And if I remember correctly you were only telling me on the bus there how I should accept Karl's proposal.'

'What point?'

'Huh?'

'What point was Evelyn trying to make?'

'That you're going to break my heart, just like you did the first time around.'

He looks away, shaking his head slowly. 'You know I never meant to do that all those years ago. Things were...complicated.'

He's telling me.

'Look, whatever happened all those years ago is in the past.'

He nods in agreement.

'But right now, you're showing me that you don't give a shit about me and are out for anything you can get. Were you serious when you said you wanted me to rethink Karl's proposal? Do you want to get rid of me now that you've had your fun?'

His face drops and he stoops slightly as if I've punched him in the stomach. 'You really think that? You really think that I'm just after sex with you?'

'Well, what else could it be?' I say, my voice breaking ridiculously. Way to look like a stalker.

He frowns, the skin around his eyes bunching. 'You've never known how special you are, have you Eric?'

I blush, hating that he's worming his way back in. The charming bastard.

I sigh, as if the weight of the world is on my shoulders. 'Look, I need to know where I stand. I know we can't make this work in real life, but I want to know if we're together this holiday? As in exclusively? So we can spend the last few days knowing what the hell this is.'

He smiles. 'I'm sorry I acted like a dick. I was just trying to make you jealous. You were the one that wanted to keep it secret in the first place. I assumed you were trying to keep your options open. Or that you didn't want the others to know.'

'I didn't,' I admit. 'The minute they hear about this the ribbing will start and there's no point before we know what's going on. So...what is it...you know, that we're doing?'

He takes my hand, a shy smile gracing his lips. 'This holiday you're mine.'

How is it that four little words can make me so happy?

I nod, grinning like a loon. 'And you're mine too?' I clarify. 'No blonde bimbos?'

He raises one eyebrow and points back towards the bar. 'You honestly think girls like that interest me?'

I shrug, still feeling insecure. 'Maybe.'

He shakes his head, rolling his eyes. He takes my hand and pulls me closer. 'What are you like?' he chuckles, wrapping his arms around my waist.

I feel a thrill go through me. He doesn't like those girls. He wants a real woman, like me. Even if only for this holiday.

He slams his lips against mine with such force that we both walk backwards until I hit the side of the coach, some kind of button pressing into my back.

Pssh, comes a sound to my right.

We both look round to see that the coach doors have opened. I must have pressed against the open switch. Jack's face lights up like a kid at Christmas. He wiggles his eyebrows suggestively, mischief dancing in them.

'Shall we?'

A thrill of excitement goes through me. 'We shall.'

He leads me onto the bus and down to the back seats. He sits down, pulling me onto his lap.

'Come here,' he says, beckoning me with his finger.

I lean forward slightly. His hands delve into my hair, pulling me into an urgent kiss. He grasps and pulls urgently, my lady bits lighting up in excitement.

His tongue teases mine, sending a tingle all down my

spine. He breaks contact to lick down my neck. His hands reach behind me and unzip my dress. Be still my thudding, thumping heart.

He pulls my dress and strapless bra down, taking a nipple in his mouth, suckling on it so tenderly I arch my back. His fingers push up my dress, finding their way into my knickers. They're pushed aside before he plunges two fingers inside me. That's obviously becoming his signature move.

A chill that has nothing to do with the weather makes me shiver. I groan like a wanton whore. I need him now. My fingers find the button of his jeans, ripping them open and pulling down the zipper. I grab him in my hand and start pumping his velvety soft skin.

'Do you have a condom?' I whisper into his ear. At least I remembered to ask this time.

'Yeah,' he says, his voice shaky. He pulls one out of his pocket and sheaths himself in record time. Someone's eager.

He rips off my knickers, sniffs them like the pervert he is and then helps me straddle him. I ease myself down onto him, my eyes practically rolling to the back of my head. It feels wonderful.

I start slow, but he quickly takes over, impaling me on him with no mercy. Before long we're both hot, sweaty and close.

I shudder with the intensity of the sensations as his hand glides over my thigh tenderly. I throw my head back as my body writhes around of its own accord, transporting me to a planet of awesome.

The noise of chatter coming closer to the bus pulls me out of my ecstasy. Shit, they're coming back. I look back to Jack, panicked.

'Shit.'

We readjust our clothes just in time for people to start boarding the bus. Damn enthusiastic bastards. I settle myself down next to him and quickly comb through my hair with my fingers. No matter which position I use it always gets messed up and sex hair always gives me away.

Jack puts his arm around me. 'You ready for this? For everyone to know?'

I smile back up at him, feeling nothing but love. 'You betcha.'

Tom and Brooke are the first ones to pass us.

'Evelyn's coming,' Brooke hisses, obviously wanting to warn us.

'It's cool,' Jack says, 'we're making it public.'

'Wait, you two?' Tom says, looking between us with furrowed brows.

'Catch up, Tom,' Charlie chuckles, barging past him. 'Like, so two days ago.'

Molly and Alice turn to stare at Charlie then back at us.

'No way!' Alice shouts, swaying from side to side, clearly drunk.

'You make such a cute couple!' Molly sings, hugging Charlie. 'Aren't they adorable!'

'Isn't who adorable?' Evelyn asks from further down.

My entire body tenses. Here we go. Jack gives a reassuring rub onto my back.

'Good luck,' Brooke whispers, moving to sit in front of us quickly.

The moment she spots us I can see she knows. She quickly looks away and attempts to ignore us. I hate when she does the ignoring, *I haven't seen you* kind of thing!

'Evelyn!' Brooke shouts, demanding her attention.

She looks over us to Brooke. 'Yes?'

'What do you think of Jack and Erica getting together?' she asks, mischief in her eyes. She wants to get a reaction. I suppose better to get it out of the way now than let it drag onto tomorrow.

She looks me dead in the eye. *'Ecstatic,'* she drawls sarcastically before averting her gaze and finding a seat.

'Well, that went better than expected,' Jack whispers in my ear.

Chapter 16

Tuesday

Erica

It was so nice to be able to spend the night with Jack without having to sneak around. Brooke slept somewhere else to give us some space. Apparently she slept in Tom's room again. *Insert eye roll here.* That girl cannot be tamed.

It's so lovely to sit next to Jack on the bus and not worry about people sussing us out. He has his arm loosely around my shoulder. Every now and again he strokes the back of my neck, playing with the loose strands of hair that didn't get collected in my top knot. I keep shivering, goosepimples appearing along my arms.

Today we're going on an excursion to see a waterfall. Apparently, there's some kind of old wives tale that if you swim under it you'll be blessed with love in abundance. I know this is only a holiday fling, but it doesn't stop me wanting to drag Jack underneath it just in case.

I'm already feeling gloomy about when we have to say goodbye to each other. But every time I think about it I shake my head, pull myself together and remind myself that this comes as no shock to me. I knew it would never work out. We have to enjoy it while we can.

The bus pulls up a dirt road and a few minutes later comes to a stop outside what looks like a jungle—lush green trees hiding any signs of a waterfall.

'Follow me everyone,' our tubby tour guide calls. We'll be lucky if he doesn't keel over from a heart attack on the way.

Jack takes my hand and guides me off the bus. I love my hand being in his...far too much. *Sigh.*

'Now,' tubby tour guide says, 'please be careful in the jungle. There are some lizards around, so be careful where you step. Respect the environment.'

Lizards? I'd better not see a lizard or I'll freak the fuck out.

'Respect the environment?' Jack whispers into my ear in amusement. I can feel the smile.

'Yeah, fuck that,' I whisper back. 'If I see a lizard I'll be screaming and running a mile.'

He grins. 'Don't worry,' he whispers back into my ear. 'I'll protect you.' A thrill goes up my spine as his breath caresses my ear.

'Woo! Let's go!' Molly shouts from near the front, as enthusiastic as ever.

We look at each other and burst out laughing. The tubby tour guide pushes some leaves apart to get into it and everyone starts piling in. Once we are inside it's like another world. Trees bigger than my house tower over us and the sounds of the jungle take over. I can hear the chirps of birds, or is that crickets? I'm not sure, but I find myself clinging to Jack's t-shirt regardless. Everyone's *oohing* and *aahing* over how fantastic it is and I'm over here freaking out.

We hike through the dry mud, trees slapping me in the face at every turn. It reminds me of *I'm a Celebrity, Get Me Out of Here.* I always assumed that was fake, but looking at this now it could be real. I'm sure my mum has that plant in her lounge.

'Be careful,' the tour guide shouts from ahead. 'It gets a bit...' His voice becomes muffled.

'What did he say?' I ask Jack, completely out of breath.

He shrugs. 'No idea.'

We've lagged a bit behind the others due to me being seriously unfit. I really need to add some cardio to my life.

'We should hurry up.' It's so much darker in here

without the sunlight filtering through. 'I don't fancy getting lost in here.'

I quicken my pace, checking my trainers for lizards.

'I don't know,' he says from behind me, 'I wouldn't mind getting lost in here with you.'

I swivel to laugh in his face and openly swoon at how utterly gorgeous he is, but lose my footing. Before I have a second to contemplate what's happening my leg is swinging behind me. The air swooshes past my face and then I'm face down. I push my face up, my hands squelching in thick, wet mud. Ugh, I thought the ground was dry around here?

'Shit,' Jack shouts, his arms under my shoulder, pulling me up. The minute he sees my face a grin explodes onto his. 'Shit.' He doubles over laughing hysterically.

'What's so funny?' I demand, trying to wipe some of the mud off my face.

'Sorry, but if you could see yourself.' He doubles over again. 'You're covered in it!'

What a way to make me feel better about almost killing myself. I mean, if the mud wasn't there I could have easily broken my nose.

I cross my arms over my chest. 'Well, thanks for making me feel even more embarrassed than I was before.'

He stops laughing, though it looks like a serious effort. 'Come on,' he smiles. 'Let's catch up with the others and get you dunked in the waterfall.'

Jesus, why is my life such a mess?

After what feels like forever trekking, we finally find a clearing, the sun shining through in invitation. Light at the end of the tunnel springs to mind. The minute the sun hits us, relief runs through my body. We're safe. We're not going to be left out here to be eaten by ravenous lizards.

'Agh!' someone screams.

I open my eyes to see Alice looking at me in revulsion, her eyes twice the size they usually are. 'What happened to you?'

I roll my eyes, shaking my head. 'I fell in mud, *obviously*.'

Molly, Brooke and the guys are already in the lagoon swimming.

'Eww!' Molly shrieks when she spots me. 'Quick, Erica, jump in and wash that off.'

I look at the murky green water. Most people would call it beautiful as the sun shimmers atop it. I can't stop thinking about potential snakes.

'No, don't!' Brooke shouts, with a cackle. 'I don't want that shit getting into the water.'

'Gee thanks.'

Jack whips his top up and over his head, exposing his beautiful body in all its glory. It never fails to leave me drooling. He dives in, not a care in the world.

'Come on in, E,' he shouts, whipping his hair back off his face. Jesus, he's like an aftershave commercial.

That's the first time he's ever called me E. It gives me a stupid thrill. Oh, why the hell not. If only to get this shit off my face and wash away the sweat I've accumulated.

I dive in, gladly washing the crap off of me with the shockingly warm water. It's almost like a bath, only with sunshine pouring onto my face. Bliss.

Evelyn looks on distastefully, her lip curled and her nose crinkled. She's avoided me ever since last night. I've decided that I'm not going to let her mood ruin mine. I'm doing nothing wrong.

Jack takes my hand and pulls me towards the waterfall. I look up at it and take in the beauty of it. It must be three storeys high, the blue water thundering down so loudly I can't hear what Jack's trying to say to me. How can water be so beautiful and powerful? It's a sobering thought.

The closer I swim the more apprehensive I feel. This could hurt, no? The way it's pelting into the lagoon makes me think of how it'll feel on my skin. He grins back at me, apparently completely unafraid of the same thing. I take a quick, deep breath before he pulls me underneath it. The water assaults me, so powerful it almost drags me under the water. Jack pulls me further still until we're underneath it.

I open my eyes to see that we survived. It's darker and secluded here, just the kind of atmosphere I'm looking for. I lick my lips at the sight of his bronzed body dripping wet. How is he not a male model?

I ache to taste his lips again. As if reading my mind, he pulls me closer, taking hold of my face and drawing my mouth up to his. His lips are soft, but firm at the same time. He groans, my pulse leaping in response. I squirm, wrapping my arms around his neck, desperate to be even closer. If heaven exists it's right here underneath this waterfall right now.

He kisses me until I feel ready to melt with the heat burning through my body. He finally pulls back, leaving me to whimper in frustration.

'We should probably get back,' he says between laboured breaths, his voice hoarse. 'Before they start looking for us.'

'Okay,' I agree begrudgingly, still feeling dizzy from those lips.

We go back under the waterfall, again it hitting me so hard I almost fall under, finally emerging on the other side. The sun seems brighter now. Tom, Molly and Alice are looking over, their eyes wide.

'You should try it!' I wave. 'It's amazing!'

Wait, why do they look so shocked? Like they've been stunned into silence. Tom wolf whistles.

'Huh?' Jack says over my shoulder. 'Shit!'

He grabs onto my tits from behind, cupping them shamelessly.

'Jack!' I hiss, 'people are watching.'

'I'm aware,' he whispers back. 'Because your bikini top has disappeared. Again.'

Oh my god. I look down and he's right. My upper half is naked. What the fuck. I search around in the water, doing the best I can without moving Jack and exposing myself again, but I can't find it. Well this is a fucking disaster. How can this be happening again?

'What is it with your need to expose yourself?' he laughs into my ear.

We move closer to them. Molly looks on with sympathy. Do the others? No. They're too busy singing *'get your tits out for the lads!'* Fuck my life.

Chapter 17

Erica

What a magical day. Well, apart from the flashing of one's tits. It's been the kind of day you dream about. Such a once in a lifetime opportunity, and to think I spent it with my Jack, well, it just brings out a fresh blush to my skin.

'You alright there?' Jack asks me later that night in the bar.

I quickly attempt to pull myself together. 'Yeah, fine,' I smile, not daring to look him properly in the eyes for fear he'd recognise my dirty thoughts.

'Really?' he asks with humour in his voice. 'Because from the way your neck is blushing right now I'd say you're aroused.'

'What?' I can feel myself blushing more, which isn't helping. I must be the colour of a beetroot right now. *Sexy*.

'Well, you better get it while you can, gorgeous.' He winks, while I frown.

'While I can?'

'Yep,' he nods, pursing his lips together. 'I can feel a migraine coming on.'

I had no idea he suffered from migraines. Poor baby.

'I have heard that sex can help,' I lie, attempting to look as seductive as possible.

'Well then, you better meet me by the toilets.' He winks and walks away.

Is he serious? Sex in a public place? Can I do that? The thought of someone finding us is humiliating. But...god, the idea of leaving him in there is more terrifying. If the ache between my legs is anything to go by I should follow him. My legs are moving before the decision is even final.

I really shouldn't be doing this. The small voice in my head keeps wanting me to confront him about that text message fifteen years ago. It's getting louder by the second.

I find him leant against the wall, his face troubled. He doesn't look like someone desperate for sex right now.

'Are you okay?' I ask, touching his arm. I feel him flinch. What the hell is going on?

'Sorry, I've just...my migraines pretty bad. I'm going to go back to the hotel.'

'Oh.' I quickly try to look concerned, rather than disappointed that I'm not getting the D. 'Do you want me to come with you?'

'Nah, it's fine. I just need to be alone in a dark room right now.'

'Okay, feel better.'

And just like that my night is ruined.

Wednesday –

Erica

I decided as soon as he'd gone that I wouldn't be one of those pathetic girls that sulk over their man going home. Instead I threw myself all in and we ended up finishing by singing karaoke at the bar until 4am, which if I'm honest, was just because we demanded the owners let us. Sheesh, we really need to drink less.

Anyway, this morning I can't wait to see him. The guys aren't around the pool so I decide to go looking for him. He might want someone to look after him. Maybe give him an erotic massage. *I wish.*

I get out of the lift and walk towards his room. I'm just turning the corner when I see his door open. I smile, glad to see him. I go to wave, but stop dead in my tracks when instead a blonde woman steps out, still in last night's dress.

What? I stare at her aghast, as if time has stood still. A mass of ideas swirl in my head. That's why he went home early last night. He's bored of me. He's had his fill and now he's moved onto the next victim. He hasn't changed at all; he's just a cold hearted bastard.

But wait, it has to have been Charlie's one night stand. Not his, right? Of course I'm right. I'm going to feel pretty silly in a minute when he steps out with her.

'Thanks again,' she coos, leaning against the doorframe.

It lets me see him. Jack. In just his boxer shorts, his chest bare. Holy fuck. It's like a bullet to the heart. I crouch down, wanting to be as small as possible as my love for him shatters into a million pieces. He slept with another woman. Holy fuck.

'Anytime,' he smiles coolly.

It's like a punch to the stomach, winding me temporarily. I stumble, falling on my knees. I blink a few times, tears escaping from my eyes.

'Erica?'

Shit, I must have made a noise. I look up to see his face as white as a ghost, looking between me and the woman in panic. Well, he obviously never thought he'd get caught. Heartless bastard.

I quickly gather myself up and run. I sprint as fast

as I can, hearing his footsteps gaining on me. I reach my room, for once that annoying card thingy working and I manage to slam the door in his face just in time.

'Erica, please! It's not what it looks like.'

'Oh, that's original,' I snort, sliding down the door to sit on the floor. The tears are flowing freely now. I'm the worst crier. I can avoid crying for years and then once I start it's hard to stop.

'Please, just let me in!' he pleads. 'I have a maid giving me funny looks. I'm pretty sure she's going to call security any minute.'

'You want me to feel sorry for you? Are you for real?'

I open up the door in my anger, leaving the chain on. 'How could you do this to me Jack? We promised we'd be together this holiday and you couldn't even keep it in your pants for one week! Is that why you left last night? So, that you could meet that slag and shag her all night. Well, I hope it was worth it.'

I slam the door, but he puts his hand in the way. His face contorts in pain. 'FUUUUUUCK!'

Shit, I might have broken his hand.

'Oh my god, are you okay?' Damn, now I sound concerned, when I should still be pissed.

'Hand! Hand!' he says in short spurts.

For fuck's sake!

I open the door and lead him into the bathroom,

running the cold tap and sticking his hand underneath it, not giving him any eye contact the entire time.

'Don't think for a second this is me thinking your behaviour is acceptable,' I snap, by now my voice is wobbly instead of sharp. It's pretty obvious to anyone with ears that I'm more hurt than angry.

He sighs, exasperated. 'Erica, this is just a stupid misunderstanding. I never slept with that woman. Tom did!'

I scoff and roll my eyes. 'Yeah, right. Tom who doesn't even share a room with you.'

'He does!' he shouts, attempting to catch some eye contact. '"Tom and Charlie swapped because Charlie's snoring was driving me mad.'

Oh. He had mentioned before that Charlie's snoring was bad. But he never told me that Charlie and Tom had swapped rooms. And that still doesn't explain why he was the one walking her out.

'So, you expect me to believe that you just slept through them having sex?'

'No, that's the point!' he snaps. 'I didn't fucking sleep at all. I still can't believe he did it. I spent half the night hiding in the toilet and the other half trying to sleep through her snoring.'

It makes me laugh to think of her snoring like a dirty little pig.

'So why were you walking her out?'

'Because, when I finally did get some sleep I woke up to find that he'd fucked off and left her there asleep. It was beyond awkward to say the least. I made her a cup of tea and apologised.'

Okay, this is sounding like something I could believe.

'Poor girl.'

He wraps his hand in a towel. 'I can't believe you thought I'd do that to you,' he says, a raw vulnerability in his eyes.

I look down, an overwhelming feeling of sadness taking over me.

'Why not? It's not like you haven't ever been a bastard to me before. Remember the text message you sent that ended us?' His face falls further. 'Yeah, well that cut me to the core and you didn't even give a shit.'

'Of course I gave a shit,' he argues with a frown.

Yeah, that's what he wants to do right now. Fight me. What an idiot.

'Then why didn't you apologise? Do you know how many years that's haunted me? I didn't lose my virginity until I was nineteen, for fuck's sake. I was terrified something was wrong with me. You made me feel like a freak. Like a too tight, frigid freak. And I don't think I'll ever forgive you for that.'

'Eric, please.' His uninjured hand reaches out for my

cheek, but I turn away. 'I was a total dick back then. I'm so sorry. I just...well, when you asked about it I felt like a complete failure. I couldn't get you aroused like in all the ridiculous porn I was watching back then.'

I snort. Guys and their bloody porn giving them unrealistic expectations.

'And...' he looks to the floor, 'I was a virgin back then too. I had no bloody idea what I was doing.'

Wait, *he* was a virgin? This is news to me.

'But...you said you'd done it before?' I can't help but ask, clutching my forehead. I have a huge headache coming on.

'I know,' he nods, smiling regretfully. 'I lied. Like I said, I was a dickhead. I have no idea why you even liked me.'

'Er, because you were *so* hot,' I joke in a silly voice.

'In my defence, I did try and call you. You never answered.'

'You called me once! Fucking once! That's hardly someone fighting to win me back.'

'I'm sorry. I was so embarrassed and I just figured if you wanted to speak to me you'd call me back. And you didn't.'

So both our prides stopped us from staying together. Well, not again. If I want to find out if we're exclusive on this holiday I'm going to have to ask.

'Well, it's just like this holiday I suppose. It's not like we've made any promises to each other.'

'I know, but...well,' he takes my hand in his uninjured one, 'it sure feels like something that we're doing, right?'

I smile, another tear falling down my cheek. 'Of course it does.'

'Only...' he runs his hand through his hair, his face clouding over again with that same look from last night.

'Only, what?'

He sighs and bites his lip. 'Only, I'm not sure I can offer you anything after this holiday.'

'Oh.' Well that's fucked me up. I know we agreed that nothing could ever happen past this week, but that doesn't mean I wasn't clinging onto the tiny possibility that something might. I try desperately not to cry, to put on a brave face in front of him. There's plenty of time once I get home to weep into my pillow. 'That's fine,' I lie with a little shrug.

He takes my head in his hands, his eyes scrunched up in pain. 'It's not that I don't want to. It's just that we lead different lives in different postcodes. We could pretend like it'll be okay, but we both know it won't work. It didn't last time.'

That doesn't mean it won't this time, I want to shout. We both drive now, we're able to visit each other without relying on our parents. But I don't want to beg. I want to hold onto the last shred of my dignity, no matter how small.

Instead I nod. 'So maybe we should just stop talking about it and enjoy our last day together?'

He tucks a stray bit of hair behind my ear. 'You're right. Do you fancy the beach? Just you and me?'

I sigh. I'm really going to miss him.

'I couldn't think of anything better.'

He smiles fondly and then winks. 'Just remember to pack a spare bikini top this time.'

Spending time just the two of us today has been bliss. The girls understood me wanting to have a selfish last day. Even Evelyn told me to have a nice time. I think she sees that I'm fully prepared to part with him tonight, whereas my fifteen year old self wasn't prepared for that outcome.

We've frolicked in the sea, borrowed some kids buckets and made sandcastles, and shared ice cream. As I lay on his chest, under our shade, stroking his chest it really hits me how unfair all of this is.

'So, your job?' I ask, deciding to be cheeky. 'It doesn't have an office in Brighton?'

He laughs, but shifts uncomfortably underneath me.

'I mean, I'd consider moving closer but I've literally *just* got this promotion. I've been working months towards it and I need to prove myself.'

I smile sadly against his chest. 'I know, I'm just being silly.'

'What about you? You don't fancy an extended holiday in Peterborough?'

I shake my head. 'My Mum's ill. I can't leave her. That's one of the reasons we came on this holiday. The girls said I needed a break.'

'Shit, I didn't know. What's wrong with her?'

'She's just finishing her last round of chemo. But she's going to be fragile for quite a while.'

'Shit, that's so sad.' He pulls me even tighter against him. I revel in the feeling of being looked after.

'Yeah, but she's absolutely fine some days. It's just made me realise I might not have as long as I think with her.'

He sighs heavily, taking my hand in his. 'I guess the world really is against us ever making a go of it, isn't it?'

I lift my head and kiss his chin. 'I think it is.' I bend down to plant a proper kiss on those delicious lips. 'Until then, I think I've seen enough of the beach. Why don't we spend the rest of the day seeing my hotel room?'

Chapter 18

Erica

I sat as close to him on the bus all the way to the airport as I could without dry humping him. I sat on his lap while we waited in the airport and now as he's just about to board the plane I can't help but feel the tears building in my eyes.

'So, this is it,' he says with a sad smile, rocking on his heels.

'I know. I just...I miss you already.' I know I sound pathetic, but it's like something has shifted between us today. We've both made it clear that in an ideal world we'd want more from each other.

He smiles and rolls his eyes, his arms wrapped around me. 'You're so bloody soppy.'

'I know. What have you done to me?'

He grins devilishly. 'It's my magic penis.'

I smile, despite feeling miserable. 'That must be it.'

I push my hand down in between us and give it a quick squeeze.

His eyes bulge out of their sockets. 'Stop!' he hisses, looking around at the others to see if they've seen. 'I can't have a boner while walking onto the plane.'

'People will just assume you're *really* into flying,' I laugh. 'Weird fetish or something.'

He rolls his eyes as if I'm ridiculous. 'I'm sure normal people wouldn't think that.'

'There are no normal people left,' I say with a wink. 'Anyway, don't go trying to join the mile high club with an eager air hostess. I'd like to think you're half as depressed as I am.'

His eyes light up with humour, but quickly dim. 'Haven't you seen Charlie today?'

I look round to see him walking towards us, clutching his stomach.

'You okay Charlie?' I ask, giving him some room.

'Ugh, I've had diarrhoea all morning. I ate some bad tacos last night. I honestly don't know how I'm gonna make it through this plane ride.'

Ah, now I get it. He'll be in and out of the plane toilet stinking it up. Hardly the kind of romantic or erotic atmosphere needed to join the mile high club. Good.

The queue moves forward until we eventually have to part.

He holds my face in his hands, smiling sadly down at me.

'Maybe one day we'll be better aligned. Until then.' He gives me a quick peck on the lips. 'It's not goodbye. It's just...see you later.' He pulls me into his chest, wrapping his arms around me as he kisses me deeply. A tear spills down my cheek. He parts to brush it away with his thumb. I smile weakly back at him. It's now or never. I'm prolonging the agony by not just biting the bullet. I push him back slowly, trying to keep my breathing under control.

He turns, handing over his boarding pass to the air hostess. He smiles back at me before turning and walking into the tunnel.

How the fuck am I going to survive without him?

Chapter 19

Jack

I knew the minute I got on that plane I couldn't live without her. But there was no point promising her anything until I'd worked out that I could definitely be with her. There are a few things I need to do. Speak to my boss and ask if a transfer is possible, and then the hard part, asking Amber and Esme what they think about it.

Erica

It's been a week. The longest week of my life. It feels so ridiculous how two weeks ago I was living the exact same life, quite content. I mean, maybe looking back, I was just bumbling along. Putting one foot in front of the other. But now it feels like there's a giant hole in my chest that only his love can fill.

And the worst thing is that he doesn't even feel the same. I mean, yes, we promised not to bother trying the long distance thing, but I guess I still kind of expected at least a text from him to say he got home safe. But no. Radio silence over here.

Brooke's gone out tonight, her usual for a Saturday. She asked me to come with her but I'm really not feeling up to it. I just want to wallow for a while, you know? Be happy in my own misery, in a weird kind of way.

I've put the washing on and I'm looking forward to settling down in front of Netflix, my pizza on order, when my phone rings. I really hope it's not someone calling with bad news. I don't have the energy for it at the moment.

I glance at the caller ID and nearly pass out when *Your Holiday Lover* flashes up. My heartbeat starts going ten to the dozen. He's calling me?

I quickly sit up straight, clear my throat and smile, as if he can see me.

'Hello?' I answer dubiously. It will be really embarrassing if he just butt-dialled me.

'Hey, Eric.' Just hearing his voice makes me want to curl up into a ball and cry over the unfairness of it all.

'Hi.'

'You already said that,' he laughs. The sound of his chuckles calms me. I fold myself up on the sofa, hugging my knees into my chest.

'Sorry, I just...you've caught me off-guard is all. I thought we said we weren't going to try and do this?'

Not that I'm not desperate to give it one last shot.

'Yeah, well I've been thinking about that.'

'Oh?' I ask, far too eagerly. Calm down Erica. Don't get too excited.

'And I think what we have is better than that.'

Oh Jesus, why is he tormenting me like this? He either wants to give it a go or he doesn't!

I sigh, suddenly exhausted and defeated by the idea of us. 'I want to try, but you know how it went last time.'

'We were teenagers last time,' he counters.

I laugh gloomily. 'I can't promise that I won't be any less immature and needy.'

The doorbell rings. At least I have my pizza to make me feel better. I knew I should have added some ice cream to the order.

'I'll take you how you are, Erica.'

I smile, despite my reservations as I swing the door open. I try to rearrange my features so I'm not grinning like a loon at the delivery boy. But that's when I see him. Jack. My Jack. At the door. My door. My jaw goes slack, hanging lifelessly.

He's got the phone to his ear, and he's also grinning like a loon. 'Surprise.'

I drop the phone on the floor and leap into his arms, flinging my legs around his waist. I press my head against his neck, inhaling him. He vibrates with a chuckle.

'I take it you're happy to see me, then?'

I lean my head back, looking into those amazing hazel eyes. 'Happy is an understatement.' I press my lips against his, savouring the taste. I never thought I'd get to kiss them again.

He walks into the flat, kicking the door shut behind him. He lays me down on the sofa, still on top of me.

'Wait.'

He stops abruptly, looking down at me. 'What? What's wrong?'

'Just...before we do this. We should sit down and talk about how it's going to happen. I mean, do you think we could see each other at least once a month?'

He grins, tucking some of my hair behind my ear. 'Didn't I tell you?'

I frown, completely confused.

'I'm moving here.'

My mouth drops open, my head spinning. 'Are you serious?'

'Yep.'

'But...what about your job? What about your promotion?'

'That's why I needed this week to speak to my boss

and get things organised. I managed to get transferred to a new Brighton office opening here. I didn't want to get your hopes up before I knew.'

'With the same position?' I ask hopefully.

'No,' he shakes his head. 'The one I was doing before the promotion, but he says that as it's new, the current manager is only there for six months setting everything up. He reckons with my knowledge I could be up for the position. He's putting a good word in for me.'

'Wow.' I still can't believe it. Are the planets really aligning for us?

'Yeah, plus he's okayed for me to have every second Wednesday off as long as I work the Saturday. And I can leave early on a Friday every second weekend.'

Well that's a bit bloody random.

'Riiiiight?' I say with a question. 'Why would you want those hours? Having a Wednesday off is a bit odd, isn't it?'

He smiles, suddenly nervous as he bites his lip. 'Well, that's where I need to sit you down and explain a few things.'

I sit up. Oh crap, what is he going to tell me? Just when I was thinking it was going well.

'Do you have a girlfriend or something?'

'Or something,' he nods. I gulp. Shit, he's married. 'I'm single, but, well...it's hard for me to explain, but...I have a kid.'

My eyes nearly bulge out of their sockets. A kid?

'You have a *what?*'

He nods. 'A daughter. She's four.'

'Oh my god. I can't believe you didn't tell me.'

He sighs, looking as if the weight of the world is on his shoulders. 'I'm sorry, but I didn't think I'd have to. Plus, I was having so much fun not having to be responsible for once. I suppose I kind of wanted to keep up the lie.'

'Jesus. Well, then you can't move here.' How can he even be considering leaving his daughter in Peterborough and moving miles away from her?

'I can. I've talked it through with Amber and Esme. I only pick her up from school every second Wednesday and have her every second weekend. With these working hours it means I'll still be able to do that. Her life won't change at all.'

'Shit.' That's when it dawns on me. Amber. 'Wait, Amber's the mum? As in...the Amber I was always jealous of?'

'That's another reason I didn't want to tell you,' he admits with a nod.

'I knew she was after you!' I shout, suddenly enraged.

'Yeah, well we were only together a month before she

told me she was pregnant. I quickly realised we couldn't be together. We split up before she was even twenty weeks. But I've always been involved with Esme. There are no hard feelings between Amber and me. We're just like friends who have a kid together.'

'How can you even be sure it's yours?'

'*It* has a name. Esme.'

I place my hand on top of his. 'I'm sorry.'

'There's no doubt in my mind.' He pulls his phone out of his pocket and scrolls through, handing it to me. On the screen is the cutest little girl I've ever seen. Big chubby, rosy cheeks, Jack's distinctive hazel eyes and brown hair. 'That's what my tattoos are about too.' He pulls up his t-shirt and points to the date. 'That's Esme's date of birth.' He points to the clock. 'That's the time she was born. She's a Leo,' he explains, pointing to the lion, 'and the elephant is because Dumbo is her favourite movie. She actually begged me to get that one.'

'I still can't believe you have a kid. And with Amber of all people!'

'Yeah, but I've kind of re-arranged my life now, so I'm really hoping you're going to come to terms with it.'

I laugh. 'I can do that.'

'Good, because I'm afraid you're stuck with me.'

I wrap my arms around his neck. 'I couldn't be happier.'

'Great, because I kind of need to move in here. Rent prices here are shocking!' He widens his eyes in mock horror.

'You want to *live* with me?' He wants to move in?

'Yeah, do you think you can handle me?' He smiles, his eyes lighting up in challenge.

'I'll give it a try.' I pull him to me and kiss him. 'But, I mean, am I really worth all of this upheaval and stress for you? For Esme?'

'Erica, you're worth the world and more. Let me spend the rest of my life making that stupid text message up to you. I can't live with anymore regrets.'

I smile shyly. The doorbell goes for the pizza. 'Be right back.'

I take the pizza and pay the delivery guy. When I bring it back in, he's kicked off his shoes and is asleep, cuddling the cushion. I look down at his angelic, sleeping face and realise that I got my happily ever after. It might have taken fifteen years, and it might not be conventional, but it's finally happened. I have my Jack.

THE END

Play List

The One That Got Away – Katy Perry
Throwback – Usher
Hypnotise – Notorious B.I.G.
Sweet Dreams – Beyonce
Seven Days in Sunny June – Jamiroquai
Wishing on a Star – Jay Z
Cool for the Summer – Demi Lovato
End of the Road – Boyz II Men
Boys Boys Boys – Grace
September Song – JP Cooper
I'm in Love with a Monster – Fifth Harmony
Run the World (Girls) – Beyonce
I'm Yours – Jason Mraz
My Boo – Usher & Alicia Keys
Count on Me – Bruno Mars
Summer Love – One Direction
Beautiful Goodbye – Maroon 5
Still Be Lovin' You – Damage
Perfect – Ed Sheeran

http://spoti.fi/2plUZWQ

Want to find out what happens with Brooke? Click below to tell Laura you want the second book.

http://bit.ly/2q8BYIl

Acknowledgements

Thank you so much for taking the time to read my book. Reviews mean so much to us indie authors, so I'd really appreciate a quick review on amazon/Goodreads.

Thank you first of all to my family for their continued support. That means me being a sleep deprived zombie mum, unable to form a complete sentence and having to take naps to keep up with my crazy writing hours. It can't be easy living with that!

Thank you to Andrea M Long for her speedy and accurate editing. Her suggestions made the book all it could be. She has mad skills!

Hart & Bailey Design pulled another one out of the bag with this beautiful cover. I just love it!

Thank you to all the readers and bloggers who take time out of their crazy schedules to share my posts and help spread the word. Without you I'd be nothing.

Special thanks to my Indie author friends that are constantly there for me when I need a rant/share/funny message. You guys rock.

Check out Laura's other titles

The Debt & the Doormat Series

The Debt & the Doormat

The Baby & the Bride

Porn Money & Wannabe Mummy

Standalones

Tequila & Tea Bags

Dopey Women

Sex, Snow & Mistletoe

Heath, Cliffs & Wandering Hearts

Adventurous Proposal

Connect with Me

www.laurabarnardbooks.co.uk

www.facebook.com/laurabarnardbooks

https://twitter.com/BarnardLaura

https://www.instagram.com/laurabarnardauthor/

Lightning Source UK Ltd.
Milton Keynes UK
UKOW06f0447100617
303029UK00001B/6/P

9 780995 655423